THE BAFFLER NUMBER TWELVE

BLOOD

T. C. Frank *Cold Kicking It With*

Rebecca Bohrman *Chicago:* 7

Christian Viveros-Faun

Pierre Bourdieu and Loïc W. *te* 69

Jim Arndon

Sandy Zipp *Shop* *science* 110

Christian Parenti *at Keynesianism* 120

AND TAILFINS

Stephen Duncombe *The Caddy That Tanks* 37

Brishen Rogers *A Different Kind of Exploitation* 41

Bryant Urstadt *Fine Scandinavian Leather* 47

IN THE REPUBLIC OF TASTES

Berlatsky, Millet, Newirth *Books* 85

Mike O'Flaherty *The Punk Escadrille* 98

Corrida Única: Jay Rosen vs. T. C. Frank 116

ART

Patrick Welch Cover

Lisa Haney 39, 41, 50-59

Hunter Kennedy 78

Le Mule 79

Brian Chippendale 96, 120-128

Jay Ryan 100, 104, 109

FICTION

Johnny Payne *I'm OK, Eeyore OK* 33

Thomas Beer *from In the Country of the Young* 63

POETRY

Pam Brown *Not the Town* 46

Dale Smith *5:30 P.M.—Friday* and *Doppio* 62

Joshua Clover *Rue Des Blancs Manteaux* 97

OBJECTIVE

Ed Debevic's Costume and Character Guide 25

Ethnic Technologies 82

The
BAFFLER

Publisher
Greg Lane

Associate Publisher
Emily Vogt

Editor
Thomas Frank

Managing Editor
"Diamonds" Dave Mulcahey

Editor-at-Large
Matt Weiland

Poetry Editors
Damon Krukowski, Jennifer Moxley

Contributing Editors
Kim Phillips-Fein, Tom Vanderbilt,
Chris Lehmann

Hodakting Editors
George Hodak, Jim McNeill

Founding Editors
Thomas Frank, Keith White

THE BAFFLER wishes to thank Gwenan Wilbur, Reg Gibbons, Michael Szalay, Eric Guthey, Serge Halimi, Dn Ptrmn, Rebecca Bohrman, Jennifer Farrell, Robert Nedelkoff, and Kristen Lehner.

We completed this BAFFLER in March, 1999. Subscriptions to THE BAFFLER cost $24 for four issues and can be purchased by check at the address below, or by credit card at thebaffler.org and 1-888-387-8947. The editors invite submissions of art, fiction, and essays. All submissions must be accompanied by a stamped, addressed envelope. Submissions should be addressed to the Editor and not to individuals. Unsolicited poetry submissions will not be considered or returned. All requests for permissions and reprints must be made in writing to the Publisher. Six weeks advance notice is required for changes of address.

All correspondence should be sent to the address below.

The selection from Thomas Beer's unpublished novel *In The Country of the Young* is from the Beer Family Papers, and appears here with the kind permission of Manuscripts and Archives, Yale University Library.

Look for these books by BAFFLER contributors: Thomas Geoghegan's *The Secret Lives of Citizens* is out now from Pantheon; Christian Parenti's *Lockdown America: Police and Prisons in the Age of Crisis* is due out from Verso in June 1999; a book of David Berman's poems is due out soon from Open City; and Lydia Millet's new novel, *George Bush, Dark Prince of Love,* is due out from Simon & Schuster in January 2000.

We aren't going to apologize for the footnotes in this issue. You know why we did it. And you should count yourself lucky: What we were *planning* to do was include a whopping introduction hemming and trimming and justifying and hedging; distancing ourselves from this and identifying ourselves with that; and then going on to gently offer direction in interpreting the essays to come because, as you know, all texts are always at least potentially multifunctional and we didn't want there to be any mistake about how we were going to discuss just one little tiny part of the thingamee and not the entire damn thingamee. Of course you'll probably think that anyway. So with a sigh we can now get started on the never-tiresome subject of how persecuted and downtrodden we are, which we were reminded of by the sight of all the sad elm tree stumps lining Fifty-ninth Street one night as we crawled home from another dispiriting editing session characterized more by interaction with a bottle of Cutty/S/ark than with any less liquid text you might mention, but which subject we will now abandon to discuss the more uplifting theme of how we persisted anyway and how we eventually subverted those hierarchies, those senseless and arbitrary walls between disciplines, between bodies of knowledge—pleasure-loving bodies, that is, bodies that the new conservatives have to regulate in order to reestablish the discipline—how we interrogated those who hoped to erect one last red-baiting barrier to difference and the threat of derision, how we intervened in their attempt to police the boundaries, and how we carefully, slowly, painstakingly circled our way around to introducing the plane of desire (and that of pleasure), which we hereby do finally do.

P.O. Box 378293, Chicago, Ills. 60637
thebaffler.org

New Consensus for Old

THOMAS FRANK

THE prominent sociologist Herbert Gans had been writing about popular culture and its audiences for some twenty years when he published his 1974 book *Popular Culture and High Culture*, a 159-page summary of his thinking on the subject. The volume is now twenty-five years old, and it builds on arguments Gans had been making since the Fifties, but if not for a number of wrong predictions and an antiquated jargon it could just as easily have been written yesterday, so reliably does it rehearse the basic scholarly prejudices that now inform the discipline known as "cultural studies." For Gans, as for so many academic critics today, the debate over high culture and mass culture nearly always concealed a broader clash between elitism and populism, between the snobbish tastes of the educated and the functional democracy of popular culture. Gans began the book, as the followers of cultural studies continue to preface theirs, by rejecting the idea "that popular culture is simply imposed on the audience from above." He describes the power of audiences to demand and receive, through the medium of the market,

the culture of their choosing from the entertainment industry, and, in what has since become the trademark gesture of cultural studies, he hammers the critics of the entertainment industry as nabobs of "elitist" taste "unhappy with [recent] tendencies toward cultural democracy." Dwight Macdonald is duly castigated for his disdain of popular intelligence, as is Herbert Marcuse, late of the famous "Frankfurt School" of Marxist social theory.

Up to this point Gans seems to have anticipated with uncanny accuracy the issues, the preconceptions, and even the enemies that would define academic literary and cultural criticism in our own time. But his streak of prescience ends abruptly when he predicts that the mass culture critique he identifies with Macdonald and Marcuse would stage a triumphant return in the very near future. Gans comes to this odd prediction by connecting the mass culture critique, as a theory that celebrates the transcendent worth of a canonical education and good taste, with the interests of intellectuals generally: When their "status" is under attack or in decline, they revert naturally to the old elitism, dreaming up all sorts of bushwa about art and culture in order to reinforce the hierarchies that support their exalted social position. But when respect for intellectuals is on the rise, they can lighten up, make peace with middle America, and watch TV along with the rest of us.

It's certainly true that, as the humanities and social sciences have recently come under the fiercest attack they have endured in generations, the barriers separating them from the world beyond have risen to unprecedented heights: Think of the clotted, ciphered academic prose that seems to knot itself more egregiously still with each blustering right-wing tirade about "tenured radicals" or half-witted crusade against "political correctness." What Gans got wrong is that the object of all this credential-flashing, sentence-mangling expertise has not been the sanctity of high culture, but exactly the opposite. The mass culture critique that Gans so abhorred has in recent years been neatly dispatched to that special oblivion reserved for intellectual anathema. Meanwhile, today's most celebrated academic figures—the captains of cultural studies, or the "cult-studs," as a star-struck reviewer once dubbed them—are, like Gans himself, unremittingly hostile to elitism, hierarchy, and cultural authority; they express reverence for the wisdom of audiences

and for the "agency" of the consumer. British critic Jim McGuigan has described this central article of the cult-stud's faith as a formulaic "populist reflex," a moral calculus in which the thoughts, proposals, or texts in question are held up to this overarching standard of judgment: What does this imply about the power of the people? Accounts of popular culture in which audiences are tricked, manipulated, or otherwise made to act against their best interests are automatically "elitist," as cult-stud commodore Lawrence Grossberg once put it (in a line echoed in almost every cultural studies essay or book I have ever read), because they assume that audiences are "necessarily silent, passive, political and cultural dopes." Cult-studs routinely characterize this "elitist" position by ascribing it to the same easy-to-hate Frankfurt School Marxists that so pissed off Herbert Gans, seeing in their work the specter of scholarly snobberies past. In reaction to the uptight squareness of the Frankfurters (one of whom, we are eternally reminded, disliked jazz), the cult-stud community wastes no opportunity to marvel at the myriad sites of "resistance" found in TV talk shows, rock videos, shopping malls, comic books, and the like. Cultural studies tracts describe the most innocent-looking forms of entertain-

ment as hotly contested battlegrounds of social conflict, wrested from their producers by freedom-minded audiences. The populist reflex has proven irresistible to U.S. academics, ever anxious to establish their down-with-the-people bona fides. And as the cult-studs began to eclipse the honchos of historicism and the dudes of deconstruction in English and American Studies departments across the land, the populist reflex spawned an academic growth industry of vast proportions. In academic publishing the number of cult-stud titles has mushroomed so suddenly and so dramatically that, by some accounts, the works of competing disciplines (namely sociology) have been forced into relative decline. Journalists who have absorbed the populist reflex call on readers to rally around the communitarian teachings of the Teletubbies or wonder whether anyone even has the right to dislike the Spice Girls.

But while the cult-studs have enshrined their curious brand of populism as the pedagogy of choice in recent years, hounding the mass culture critique from the field and establishing their notions of agency and resistance as interpretative common sense, neither Gans nor anyone else from the sociological school with which he is identified was invited to the victory party. Gans's 1974 book may have been a direct antecedent of the bumper crop of cult-stud monographs and anthologies published by Routledge in the last ten years, but you will search those books in vain for references to Gans and his colleagues. This is especially curious given the cult-studs' near-compulsive reciting of influences and intellectual genealogy. Gans is not mentioned in either the vast bibliography or the index of the gigantic 1992 anthology *Cultural Studies*; he does not appear at all in Patrick Brantlinger's 1990 history of cultural studies, in Lawrence Grossberg's 1992 version of the history of cultural studies, in Stanley Aronowitz's 1993 account of cultural studies' history, in Simon During's 1993 anthology on the history of cultural studies, in John Fiske's 1993 book on cultural studies and history, in Angela McRobbie's 1994 version of the history of cultural studies, in Jeffrey Williams's 1995 anthology on the culture wars and cultural studies, or in Cary Nelson and Dilip Gaonkar's 1996 anthology on academia and the history of cultural studies.

Andrew Ross, almost alone among leading cult-studs, admits not only that the present-day conflict between elitist dupe-theories and audience-agency notions has been going on in the United States since the Fifties, but that the populist promontory he and his colleagues now hold is one they inherited from sociologists of that era like Gans and David Riesman.[†] But even those cult-studs who acknowledge the non-novelty of the populist reflex offer militant defenses of their discipline's uniqueness. Not on the grounds of its methods or theories, which draw on a range of influences, but on the grounds of politics. Cult-stud potentate Simon During fired the first shot in Routledge's 1993 offensive by distinguishing cultural studies from all other forms of academic criticism on grounds that it is "an engaged discipline," a proudly

---

[†] Andrew Ross has followed Gans in other ways as well, reportedly moving to Disney's planned suburb of Celebration, Florida much as Gans once moved to Levittown, New Jersey in order to study the unfairly maligned suburbanites who lived there.

committed leftist scholarship. Cultural studies has in fact produced a great number of powerful and enlightening works of scholarship, and many of the discipline's adherents sincerely embrace left politics. At their worst, however, the cult-studs' radical chest-thumping (of the type that seems to be a mandatory element in the long introductions to their treatises, which ring with claims to stand at the very vanguardiest of the van) tends only to draw attention to their actual distance from politics as it's experienced outside the academy. In that outside world, of course, the Nineties have been a disastrous decade for the left, a time of surrender and defeat on issues from deregulation to welfare to health care. But cultural studies has prospered extravagantly ever since that moment in 1990 when Stuart Hall, delivering the keynote address at one of the discipline's founding conferences, thrilled the assembled cult-studs with talk of imminent "institutionalization." Today it dominates the liberal arts as no pedagogy has since the height of the Cold War, its notions of audience agency and the omnipresence of resistance as emblematic of the Nineties academy as Arthur Schlesinger's "vital centrism" was of Fifties scholarship. As such it begs to be evaluated critically in its own right.

We might begin by asking about the curious absence of Herbert Gans from the swinging, resistance-filled world of the cult-stud. One suspects the answer to this puzzle lies first of all in his politics: Although Gans has been a refreshing voice of common decency on the question of wel-

fare "reform," one senses that rallying to the defense of the welfare state is far too pedestrian an intervention for the new breed of radical. Certainly Gans is not overlooked because his books are out of print: On the contrary, many of them (most notably *The Levittowners*, his famous 1967 defense of suburbia) are still well known to encomiasts of middle America like Alan Wolfe and Joel Garreau. Perhaps it is this very appeal, and Gans's consensus credentials generally, that explain his absence from the cult-stud stable. Gans came from an intellectual generation that (to simplify ruthlessly) tended, in the face of a terrifying Cold War enemy, to downplay social conflict in order to emphasize a vision of a healthy and well-functioning national whole. In books like Daniel Bell's *The End of Ideology* and Richard Hofstadter's *The Age of Reform* the consensus scholars (no studs they) portrayed dissent as disease; in public places like *Partisan Review* they more or less abandoned their adolescent leftism and enlisted in the American Century.

Today we can imagine nothing more reprehensible. The very idea of consensus is intellectual poison for us, dismissed in the modish reaches of academia as an article of Cold War propaganda and denounced as quasi-fascist in épater-by-numbers fare like the movie *Pleasantville*. In the works of the cult-studs the consensus era comes off as a time of scholarly practice so degraded it is scarcely worth remembering. By contrast, any proper cult-stud is out to develop, as Henry Giroux once put it, "a radical politics of difference," to revel in cultural and identity fragmentation, to pose boldly on the ramparts of the culture wars, to provoke and savor the denunciations of half-witted fundamentalists.

Given such a gloriously transgressive, decentering present, it seems simply inconceivable that the cult-studs should have anything to do with Gans and his consensus crowd. No, they must have an intellectual lineage more in keeping with their status as the *ne plus ultra* in counterhegemony, and so when the occasion arises (as it does so very, very frequently) to track their pedigree, the cult-studs nearly always claim descent not from the plodding drayhorses of American sociology but from the purest-blooded of barricade-charging European stallions.[†]

Still, the ghost of consensus will not rest. We may hear how the cult-studs stand on the front lines of political confrontation; we may gape at the wounds inflicted by the reactionaries upon their noble corpus; but we cannot help noticing that the noise from the front sounds a lot like somebody shaking a big chunk of sheet metal just behind the curtain.

II.

WHILE there is no denying that a number of very vocal right-wingers are driven to apoplectic fury by the cult-studs' assaults on hierarchy—and that in this sense the champions of the popular do indeed "fight the power" as they like to believe—it is also worth pointing out that they share with their foes the same imagined *bête noir*. In February Moral Majoritarian Paul Weyrich fixed the blame for the demise of "Judeo-Christian civilization" on the same gang of sneaking German reds so demonized by the cult-studs (Weyrich singled out Herbert Marcuse in particular). But leaving aside the scattershot lunacy of the Christian right and comparing the populist reflex to the faction of the American right still in possession of something like sanity, one finds the cult-studs' particular species of transgression trangresses a lot less than all their talk of "radical politics of difference" would imply.

---

† The willingness of those Europeans, especially the Birmingham School, to acknowledge American sociology is a different matter entirely. See Dick Hebdige, *Subculture*, pp. 75–79, and Ken Gelder and Sarah Thornton, eds., *The Subcultures Reader* (Routledge, 1997). Another factor in Gans's disappearance is his well-known hostility to "postmodernists" in sociology who, as Gans recently put it in a letter to *The Nation*, insist on downgrading class as an analytic concept out of a curious revulsion against "long-gone vulgar and Stalinist Marxisms."

Rat Choice and Other Tastes

Rebecca Bohrman

Perhaps the most annoying conceit of neoclassical economics is that it alone, among the social sciences, comprehends human behavior, and does so in a way that makes perfect sense to the man in the street. Sociologists and anthropologists may come up with more or less interesting (if ad hoc and atheoretical) ways to describe society and culture, but they just don't grasp the all-encompassing power of individual agency. The neoclassical economist, however, believes that economic, political, and social outcomes are the result of choices made by individuals maximizing their expected utility. People have stable, ranked preferences for, say, wealth and security, and they select the presidential candidate, job, or neighborhood that they believe will best maximize their income and safety. Sound a little reductionist? Maybe that's because you need to come down a peg or two. "People who are not intellectuals," sniffs rational choice guru Gary Becker, endorse the "rational choice approach" instinctively.

Critics have pointed out that rational choice theory wrongly assumes that things like tastes are given and stable, and that much of human behavior is affected by irrational factors such as habits, addiction, culture, and norms. But Becker will have none of this. **Accounting for Tastes**, his 1996 collection of essays, argues that rational choice theory can indeed predict seemingly irrational behavior, as well as explain tastes. Explaining why people want what they want has traditionally been beyond the pale for economists, who, probably for good reason, stuck to figuring out how people get what they want. Becker, however, is a Nobel laureate, a former economic policy advisor to Bob Dole, and the baddest of the Chicago Boys. He's never met a subject that couldn't be flattened by the analytic steamroller of free-market theory: Rising divorce rates are caused by lax no-fault divorce laws, which lower the incentive to invest in love; discrimination occurs when racist employers willingly pay a premium to employ white workers. Taste, it turns out, is just as easily accounted for. To a certain extent, our preferences are determined by "childhood and other experiences, social interactions, and cultural influences." We're also free, to the extent we can afford it, to choose our own poison, whether it's speculating in Furbies, smoking crack, or listening to postrock.

But if tastes were irreducibly subjective, then predicting behavior would be impossible—and Becker's musings on the subject would have all the authority of, say, phrenology. No, Becker needs a calculus of stable, universal "meta-preferences" that applies to CEOs and Indian peasants alike. These meta-preferences, also known as the "extended utility function," encompass desires for goods (like health or shoes), "personal capital" (past experiences), and "social capital" (peer pressure, desire for esteem, and the like). In other words, you might want to buy a Land Rover because you live in the veldt, or because you grew up in the veldt, or because your buddies at work think it would really kick ass to off-road through the veldt. Wait—sorry—that's the "sport utility function." In any case, a troublesome question dogs Becker's theory: Do meta-preferences exist, and if they do, how can we tell what they are? You'll have to take Becker's word—like subatomic particles or the **chupacabra**, "utilities cannot be observed."

Meta-preferences may be invisible, but they sure are useful. Since deep

To an undeniable degree, the official narratives of American business—expressed in advertising, in management theory, in pro-business political and journalistic circles—largely share the cult-studs' oft-expressed desire to take on hierarchies, their tendency to find "elitism" lurking behind any criticism of mass culture, and their pious esteem for audience agency. Here, too, from the feverish epiphanies of *Fast Company* to Condé Nast's breathless reverence for celebrity, a populist reflex dominates the landscape. Here, too, all agree that we inhabit an age of radical democratic transformation; that we can no longer afford slow, top-down organizational models, tyrannical bosses, or cringing subalterns; that no error, moral or intellectual, outranks elitism, the conviction of regulators, critics, and European bureaucrats that they know better than the market or the audience. Here, too, the language and imagery of production has been effaced by that of consumption; class by classism; democracy by interactivity, with the right of audiences to "talk back" to authors (usually via the Web but also through focus groups, polls, and the heteroglossia of brands) trumping all other imaginable rights and claims. It's a world where "meta offices" are presided over by heroic "change agents" seeing to it that we are all "empowered." Where the old-fashioned leftist suspicion of mass culture is used endlessly as evidence of a distasteful leftist "elitism" generally: a stereotype that has become increasingly commonplace as the arbiters of American culture fall in behind the idea of the market as a pure expression of the popular will. A recent *New York Times* article on the visiting prime minister of Italy, for example, highlights his "hauteur" and "disdain" for the tastes of common people (he has "a dim view of American popular culture") as a way of explaining his otherwise unimaginable left politics.

Unfortunately, it's difficult to discover what the cult-studs themselves think about the parallel world of corporate populism. Apart from a generalized hostility to business and frequent use of abstractions like "late capital," cultural studies has failed almost entirely to produce close analyses of the daily life of business. McGuigan attributes this recurring problem to "a terror of economic reductionism," a pervasive intellectual reflex that, out of their aversion to explaining people's actions in terms of class, leads cult-studs to steer clear of the problem altogether. One wants to avoid reductionism, naturally, but why, wonders historian Eric Guthey, have "so many highly trained, intelligent and critical cultural scholars . . . chosen to overlook so completely the burgeoning corporatization of American culture?" At a time when corporations boast of being related to God and when Microsoft reminds millions of people every day of the meaning of domination, he asks, "isn't this a bit like oceanographers refusing to acknowledge the existence of water?"

There still exist, of course, many species of cultural study that neither ignore the corporate world nor suffer from rampant reductionism. Erik Barnouw, for example, while doing close readings here and there, still managed to spend a very distinguished career evaluating the broadcasting industry as a business enterprise granted specific franchises by the government; Roland Marchand dissected advertising and public relations with insights that arose directly from those industries' function in the world of business. In the works of the cult-stud captains, however, both are treated to the same helping of oblivion as Herbert Gans. The editors of the original *Mass Culture* anthology, published in 1957, arranged its articles according to industry and freely mixed analyses of culture as a business with studies of audience behavior. Routledge organized its massive *Cultural Studies* anthology of 1992 alphabetically by contributor's name; the book monotonously pounds home the active-audience interpretation regardless of the subject being evaluated.

It is a surprisingly short walk from the cult-studs' active-audience theorizing to the most undiluted sort of free-market orthodoxy. While the cult-studs may insist proudly on the inherent radicalism of their ideas concerning agency, resistance, and the horror of elitism, as these notions are diffused outside the academy their polarities are reversed; they come across not as daringly counterhegemonic but as a sort of apologetics for existing economic arrangements. Consider, for example, the extremely negative connotations of the word "regulate" as it is used in the cultural studies corpus: Almost without variation it refers to the deplorable actions of an elite even more noxious than the Frankfurt School, a cabal of religious conservatives desperately seeking to suppress difference. And then consider the strikingly similar negative connota-

down, we all have the same needs, meta-preferences "form a stable foundation for welfare analysis that uses Pareto-optimality." Translated from rat-choice, Becker believes that certain government policies can make everyone better off. Let's say that some people think they prefer more unemployment insurance or public health care. They suffer from a rational choice version of false consciousness; what they really want, according to Becker, is government policies that create the most "wealth" by letting the rich keep their money and taking money away from the poor to give them incentives to work harder. Strangely enough, meta-preferences always point to reduced government spending. Consider this Becker chestnut: Government social security programs make "selfish parents become meaner." In societies without the nannying encumbrance of social security, you see, parents don't hit or abuse their kids because they want nice children who will care for them when they grow old. Even when the rich get more than their share, the lower classes don't suffer. Becker provides a strange account in which the rich use churches to indoctrinate the lower classes with utility-reducing norms, such as humility and self-abnegation. But because the rich provide subsidies through the church, "no one is harmed." Oligarchy, Becker-style, is a win-win proposition; it satisfies the whims of the rich and the meta-preferences of the poor.

While Becker does at least acknowledge that people are motivated by more than pecuniary self-interest, his argument remains strikingly tautological: People prefer to get what they want, and we know what they want because they got it. In the end, Becker is not able to use calculus and graphs to show why, as he puts it, "some people get addicted to alcohol and others to Mozart." But we do know this: Even if some people think they want more government spending, what we all really need is laissez-faire capitalism.

tions of the word as it is used by the *Wall Street Journal,* where it also refers to the deplorable actions of an obnoxious elite, in this case liberals who assume arrogantly that they know better than the market. Both arise from a form of populism that celebrates critical audiences but that has zero tolerance for critics themselves.

Certain academics are capable of bringing the two populisms together with breathtaking ease. Economist Tyler Cowen, for example, takes advantage of the recent stature of cultural populism by translating the populist reflex into an extended pronunciamiento on the benevolence of markets. In his book *In Praise of Commercial Culture,* he flits here and there over the entire history of art, seeking always to prove that the market is the prime mover of all worthwhile cultural production. The market guarantees quality. The market guarantees diversity. And have you ever considered who pays the bills for all those artists? That's right: the market. Cowen's thesis is the kind of confirmed philistinism economists cultivate these days to tweak their colleagues in real disciplines. But dismissing it as such merely plays to his deployment of the populist reflex. As it turns out, the market maintains the strong record it does (over the centuries, according to Cowen's accounting, batting real close to 1.000) because it is indistinguishable from the people.

And "an audience," he writes, "is more intelligent than the individuals who create their entertainment." Those who recognize popular intelligence are "cultural optimists," in whose camp Cowen puts himself, Gans, and a handful of leading cult-studs, all of whom wisely believe in letting the people and the market make their decisions without interference. On the other side, meanwhile, stands a motley group of critics united only by their shared "elitism," the conviction that they know best. From the Frankfurt School (who come in for severe chastisement) to the Christian right, they are all "cultural pessimists," doubtful about the people's capacity to decide for themselves, skeptical about popular tastes, contemptuous of progress itself. As even the Nazis can be made to fit under such a broad definition of "pessimism," Cowen does so with alacrity, closing the matter decisively.

Economist Stanley Lebergott extends this model of cultural-democracy-through-markets to the economy as a whole in a *New York Times* op-ed piece that appeared last year. Absurd as it might seem to portray the global economy as an expression of the general will, it gets stranger still when Lebergott uses the handy stereotype provided him by the cult-studs' long fight against the Frankfurt School to bash critics of consumer culture generally. The specific target in this case is none other than Hillary Clinton, who made the mistake of publicly questioning our "consumer-driven culture" while at the World Economic Fo-

rum in Switzerland, and who thus brought down on herself the severest charge that the vocabularies of free market and cult-stud can muster: Elitism! Lebergott strikes a cult-studly pose as he reduces her to a cartoon snob and then bravely defies the arrogance of the "best and . . . brightest," who never hesitate to "pass judgment." Against these eggheads he counterposes a virtuous "us," the "270 million Americans" who create everything as we humbly "decide to buy." The logic of agency, which Lebergott rephrases as rational consumer choice, is here taken to its logical conclusion: Since we are active consumers, not cultural dopes (the economist sagely notes how we don't fall for every single ad), we endorse every movement of the market economy as surely as if we had voted on it. Lebergott nails the matter down by shifting his argument from the difficult stuff of economics to the now-universal populist reflex of the cult-studs, using the language of highbrow-baiting to apply the ultimate smear to those who criticize or seek to alter this global gloriosity. Asserting first that "conferences on the world economy" are only held in the resort towns of Switzerland because it is among "splendid hotels, high fashion shops and millionaires" that left-leaning elitists feel at home, he insists that only those who shop at Wal-Mart possess the right to a critical opinion. Lebergott even busts a little postcolonialism on us, suggesting that future economic summits be held in "Calcutta or Lagos," places inhabited by market-savvy real people whose distasteful presence would cause the "fine minds" to stay home.

Outside the academy the translation of cultural studies into free-market ideology is more pronounced. Granted, newspaper stories on the cult-studs rarely manage to do much more than marvel at the spectacle of people with Ph.D's writing about Barbie and "The Simpsons," but the cult-studs' trademark language of the rebel consumer has seeped down to earth nonetheless. As it descends, it mutates into the language of the culture industry, its fight against hierarchy changes into a convenient weapon to stigmatize industry critics as elitists; its war against highbrow taste slides into the hegemonic logic of demographics. And while many cult-studs only rarely participate in any kind of extra-scholarly discussion, still they do have a role to play.

A revealing glimpse of this transformation in action can be found in the November 1995 issue of *Spin* magazine, a special issue "guest edited" by Jaron Lanier, a figure renowned in computer circles from Palo Alto to Prague for having coined the term "virtual reality." Over the years Lanier has become a sort of physical embodiment of the cyber-revolution's liberating promise, mixing copiously dreadlocked, in-your-face attitude with long-winded exegeses on the industry as a vast boon for human freedom. And whether it's the cover of *Civilization* magazine or a puffy profile in *Fortune*, Lanier's dreads seem always to be the focus of gaping admiration (granted, they are unusually full and healthy-looking for a white person of his age), establishing a rock-solid hipster credibility without messy argument.[†] Among other things, he had the honor of being one of the first to outline the position on the Microsoft antitrust trial that has since become the rallying cry of the free-market right, declaring from the authoritative heights of *The New York Times* op-ed page in 1997 that it was fruitless to even *consider* applying those second-wave antitrust laws to such superadvanced organizations. Ordinarily, of course, Lanier's dreads are sufficient to certify that such ideas are not those of some hated hierarch, but occasionally better credentialling is in order. In *Spin*, therefore, he is paired with none other than prominent cult-stud bell hooks, who evidently appears solely to legitimate Lanier. In a photo hooks gazes at his dreads, and in the accompanying text she gapes in terms only slightly different from those chosen by *Fortune*: "it strikes me how radically different you are, Jaron, from the prototypical image most people have of the nerdy white man behind the computers."

It strikes other cult-studs as well. Andrew Ross, for example, finds in the transformation of the hacker "profile" from an "elitist" and "undersocialized college nerd" to a diploma-free hipster who "dresses streetwise" a veritable "counterculture." Unfortunately, the same highly visible transformation has also powered years of cyber-industry propaganda, with the dreads and 'tude of its leading figures serving so thoroughly to establish the Web as a standing challenge to authority of any kind that even defenses

of Microsoft these days are cast in anti-elitist terms. In showplaces like *Wired* and *Fast Company* the populist reflex—the fantasy of agency for everyone, of cultural democracy through electronic articulation—is very much an industry line, and the cult-studs have shown surprisingly little ability to distinguish between anti-elitism as publicity strategy and the genuine article. Emblematic of this confusion is the oddly universal reverence for cult-stud Donna Haraway, who is apotheosized with enthusiasm by both Ross and *Wired* (the latter quoting and name-checking her on a fairly regular basis). In her contribution to the landmark Routledge ur-anthology of 1992, Haraway declares herself a partisan of "socialism" but quickly distances herself from "the deadly point of view of productionism," celebrating instead a curious techno-environmentalism that emphasizes not just human agency but that of animal "actants" as well. Haraway shows herself to be a discerning reader of Eighties-style corporate culture, cleverly analyzing a number of dry computer and medical advertisements, but when it comes to the Web-based corporate fantasies of the Nineties her critical edge disappears, as she declares "to 'press enter' is not a fatal error, but an inescapable possibility for changing maps of the world, for building new collectives out of . . . human and unhuman actors." When it's an "inappropriate/d other" at the keyboard (a guy with dreads or, in Haraway's chosen example, a woman with a big

Continued on page 80

[†] *Fortune* also adds Lanier's skills with exotic instruments to the mix, commencing its story about him with an anecdote of how he played "nose flute" at "the Kitchen, the famous avant-garde nightclub in downtown Manhattan."

THE PRONOUNCED FAVORITE IN THE SMARTEST AND MOST EXCLUSIVE CIRCLES

That there are no other magazines in all the world like THE BAFFLER is eloquently confirmed by the character of THE BAFFLER clientele. Wherever the celebrated and the sophisticated gather, our covers protrude from stylish pockets. Well-coiffed heads nod discreetly over our orderly pages. Patricians prate effetely of the Culture Trust, murmur languidly about hip capitalism.

Why don't you join them? Subscriptions to THE BAFFLER are $24 for four issues. Please tell us the number with which you'd like to begin your membership (12 or 13). ❦ Consider giving THE BAFFLER as a gift. Our uniquely tasteful leftism makes it an appropriate souvenir for friends or self-improvement exercise for the help. Please remember to give us the name of the giftor as well as that of the giftee. ❦ Cut a figure with our precious irony T-shirt. Featuring the celebrated "Burnout Diptych" from issue number seven, it fondly recalls and gently derides the styles of our early Eighties youth. Available in "Jeroboam" and "Methuselah" sizes ($12). ❦ THE BAFFLER "baseball" cap: In blaze orange, with styling by Vis-mat™, just in time for grouse season ($20), or in monoxide-blue brushed cotton ($14).

The Baffler Magazine

P. O. Box 378293, Chicago, Ills. 60637 • thebaffler.org

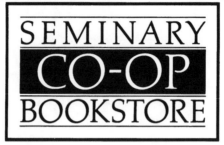

A Funny Kind of Boosterism
The Literature of "McOndo"

FIRST it was Chilean Alberto Fuguet, the author of *Mala Onda* (1991), a tale of adolescent satiety successful enough to travel northward to its alternative-spiritual birthplace and go into publication in the United States as *Bad Vibes* (1997). Then came Peruvian TV host Jaime Bayly and his best-selling novel *No se lo digas a nadie* ("Don't Tell Anyone," 1994). In Spain, it was José Angel Mañas, author of *Historias del Kronen* (1994), a trite if nervy tale which leapt from newsstands onto movie screens across Spain just a few summers after being short listed for the prestigious Nadal Prize.

Throughout the Nineties, the "McOndo" authors, as they call themselves, broke sales records, outfast-tracked the economic integration of Europe and the Americas, won the plaudits of Anglophone critics, and caused the still largely genteel world of Spanish-language publishing to echo what is without question the most noxious U.S. literary trend of the last twenty years.

Fuguet himself, a thirtysomething child of Santiago's upper-middle class and a vigorous exponent of its peculiarly provincial yet media-saturated tastes, coined the term "McOndo." As opposed to Gabriel García Márquez's magical realist "Macondo," that Latin Yoknapatawpha County populated with blue dogs and flying grandmothers, Fuguet describes McOndo as "a world of McDonald's, Macintoshes and condos." "In a continent that was once ultra-politicized," Fuguet declared in a 1997 McOndo manifesto published in *Salon*, "young, apolitical writers like myself are now writing without an overt agenda about their own experiences."

Fuguet deserves credit for pegging the present-day exponents of magical realism as purveyors of predictable, exoticized clichés, a jalapeño-popper literature dealing in "the cult of the underdeveloped" for North American audiences. But the antidote that Fuguet proposes to these Latino fairy tales is, if anything, even more compromised and derivative: Tales of jaded adolescents and urban cosmopolitanism derived forthrightly from the once-popular novels of Jay McInerney, Douglas Coupland, and Bret Easton Ellis (this last reigning as a sort of muse-in-chief for McOndo's endless evocation of sated-but-somehow-unhappy rich kids). "Kind of like *The*

House of the Spirits," Fuguet chides, "only without the spirits."

Still, Fuguet insists, multiculti habits die hard, particularly those of the U.S. literary scene. In his *Salon* essay Fuguet complains about the time he spent at the Iowa Writer's Workshop in 1994, plying a story so overwrought in its imagined victimization by the politically correct that one suspects Fuguet made it up himself: "I was invited, along with other foreign writers, to a welcome reception," Fuguet recalls, when "one of the program coordinators casually suggested it would be great to see everyone in their 'native outfits.' " Offended by his hosts' failure to recognize his cosmopolitanism instantly, Fuguet "went down in an MTV Latino T-shirt (sent to me by a VJ friend), baggy shorts and a pair of Birkenstocks. The coordinators were disappointed, to say the least."

This, then, is the whole story of McOndo in a single gesture: The poncho-wearing, bean-munching internationalism of the Iowa Writer's Program upstaged— faced!—by Fuguet's sartorially trite but more up-to-date response. Still, there's something sad about the pre-fab-hip outfit Fuguet put on to *épater* the Iowa people in their pre-alternative innocence. (How cool are Birkenstocks and an MTV T-shirt on a thirty-year-old man, anyway? How cool is it really that Fuguet *knows an MTV VJ*?) And there's something downright tragic about his guileless conviction—at least as he explains it for the readers of *Salon*—that the coolness of this stuff is simply beyond question. Fuguet's outrage at

being thought "not Latino enough" also gives us clues into what he means by the "political," a horror he pretends to flee like the Ebola virus. As Fuguet sees it, the literary world is pretty simple: There are the "Sagas of sweaty migrant farm laborers, [and] the plight of misunderstood political refugees," which he ridicules; and then there is his story of the Iowa PC police. Politics, for Fuguet, is something that happens to other people.

In North America, of course, we understand "politics" differently, and for Anglophone critics accustomed to hailing whatever sexual practices or consumer habits that irritate Jesse Helms as the latest in "subversion," the rise of Fuguet and Co. has been a radical development indeed, a triumph of the culture war politics of representation over the plodding workerist fashions of yore. Chilean writer Antonio Skarmeta has called *Bad Vibes* "a revolutionary departure from all the literary norms made fashionable by Latin American writers of the 1970s and 1980s." David Gallagher, writing for *The Times Literary Supplement*, has quite wrongly asserted that since McOndo writers "aren't writing for an international audience," they "have no need to maintain the status quo of the stereotypical Latin America that is packaged up for export."

Sadly, the truth about McOndo is that its Latin American status is all that prevents it from being summarily dismissed as the pretentious derivative of the Ellis, McInerney, and Coupland triumvirate that it is. Packed, Tarantino-like, with quotations-in-translation of everything from *Prozac Nation* to *Henry, Portrait of a Serial Killer* to the *Trainspotting* soundtrack, each of the McOndo novels chronicles the jaded anomie of the young, the beautiful, the empty, and the rich, providing exact literary analogues for the commercially sponsored alienation that serves as the bait and tackle of the late capitalist shill.

In Spain, the new authors were initially dubbed, after Mañas's 1994 bestseller, "The Kronen Generation." Narrated in an overwhelmingly narcissistic first person, Mañas's *Historias del Kronen* relates a summer in the life of a disaffected adolescent. This one's named Carlos, and he randomly drinks, smokes, snorts, and trips his way through the Madrid dawn while casually quoting pop-culture signposts and becoming as sex-addled, emotionally numb, and filled up with

repressed violence as a sunburned Big Ten fratboy at Lauderdale.

A typical Mañas ploy, for example, is to have Carlos narrate scenes from his favorite Anglophone movies when the story gets slow. "[*A Clockwork Orange*] is a classic of film violence," Carlos tells a female partner in one typically desensitized encounter. "My favorite scene is when Alex and his friends are raping the writer's wife. Alex cuts open the bitch's red suit with a pair of scissors while the others hold the writer down, forcing him to watch. Alex is belting out 'I'm Singing In the Rain' and kicks him to the beat of the music." Strangely, Mañas never describes the little punk panting and fingering his assault rifle— maybe to keep his apoliticism viable.

Historias del Kronen, like its genre-mates, shamelessly advertises its debt to American precur-

sors—in this case Ellis's 1990 novel *American Psycho*, which is not only said to be Carlos's favorite reading, but which also seems to have served as a literary model for Mañas as well, to judge by the frequency with which his characters repeat the words of Ellis's murderous protagonist. The *Kronen* kids' listening and viewing material consistently runs to Anglophilic fare as well: *Repo Man*, Nirvana, "Depesh Mod." Whether the landscape is Madrid, Santiago, or Timbuktu, it is invariably described as a generic version of a Miami suburb, full of "Pizzajat" (Pizza Hut), "Sebenileben" (7-Eleven) and bars called "Huarjols" (Warhol's).

Lucía Etxebarria, who won the prestigious Nadal Prize for her 1998 novel *Beatriz y los cuerpos celestes* ("Beatriz and the Heavenly Bodies"), is arguably the most successful member of the McOndo squad. Previously celebrated for the books *Aguanta esto* ("Take That"), a biography of Courtney Love, and *Amor, curiosidad, Prozac y dudas* ("Love, Curiosity, Prozac and Doubt"), Etxebarria fashions herself, both as a writer and public figure, as an Iberian Camille Paglia via the keening of Elizabeth Wurtzel, with the novelizing of Naomi Wolf thrown in for good measure. Irritatingly, she looks and dresses just like Tama Janowitz.

The literary model, though, seems more *Rules of Attraction* than *Less Than Zero*. The story of an adolescent whose parents just don't

Allégorie (la Mort).

seem to understand, *Beatriz y los cuerpos celestes* cuts in and out of geographies like stage sets in a music video. London, Paris, Madrid, and once-dowdy Edinburgh (Thanks Irvine Welsh! Thanks Ewan McGregor!) have never looked so similar. In these uniform cities, Beatriz tries on the various backwards baseball caps of transgression, going lesbian, trading plenty of spit and bodily fluids, partying, taking drugs, and getting violent, all the while prattling on in the easy-listening style of A. S. Byatt about love lost and found and, what else, her dear old mum and dad ("They fuck you up," you can almost hear Ted Hughes intoning throughout the book).

Indeed, one doesn't need to read too far before familiar bits begin appearing in the pulp between Etxebarria's expensive hardcovers. The first page alertly drops a reference to the whiny pop band The Cure, much as Colette might have once mentioned a Liszt sonata. The sense of leaden cliché, of ready-made irony so exhausted it would have seemed tired fifteen years ago, pops up again only a few pages further, as Beatriz narrates an exchange of postcards between herself and her brand new Scottish lover, Cat. "Cat would receive a postcard of *The Enterprise* which cost me eight francs," she relates, in what reads like Captain Kirk's overanxious voiceover. "When I returned to Edinburgh, I found in my mailbox the card Cat had promised me: a portrait of Doctor Spock. I knew then that our story was condemned to prosper." What's next, Ms. Etxebarria's high school poetry?

The most interesting proponent of McOndo is Jaime Bayly. Best known as the host of a Latino imitation of the *Merv Griffin Show*, featuring an assortment of stars from across Latin America's uniquely tacky constellation, Bayly also received Spain's Herralde Prize for his 1998 novel *La noche es virgen* ("Night Is a Virgin"). Like McOndo literature generally, Bayly nimbly straddles two worlds: He is both a master of international television cheese and a genuine auteur with a glowing critical reputation. Bayly is also where the limitations of a literature spawned by the sad-young-rich-kid narratives of Bret Easton Ellis begin to make themselves blindingly obvious. An account of South American life through the eyes of a nostalgic rich boy, Bayly's 1994 novel *No se lo digas a nadie* offers yet another look at the lives of tacky, glutted descendants of European immigrants as they shuttle in and out of exclusive restaurants, bars and country clubs, all the while casting Lima, a one-horse town if there ever was one, in the role of Proust's Paris or Fitzgerald's New York. Typical of the genre in its inability to transcend wishful thinking, Bayly imagines Lima as it might be dreamed by some liberal economist or IMF functionary. *No se lo digas a nadie* displays few traces of verisimilitude; nowhere appears the rough and shoddy, real-life Lima of gated communities and packs of beggar boys. Even the plot seems canned: In place of dramatic conflict, and following the imported lifestyle formula to the letter, Bayly locates his protagonist's principal dilemma on extremely familiar terrain—a coy, tame, and gilded homoeroticism hardly worth a solo wank.

All this helps to explain what Fuguet, the self-appointed generalissimo of the squeaky-clean McOndo bunch, means when he calls for an "apolitical" Spanish literature. It is also worth noting that Fuguet considers himself a true believer in "cultural realism"—as opposed to the realism of Victor Hugo or the Chilean novelist Manuel Rojas—"a sort of NAFTA-like writing," as he has actually called it. "This new genre," Fuguet has explained, innocently, "may be one of the byproducts of a free-market economy and the privatization craze that has swept South America."

May be? How about as surely as Fuguet lives and breathes his precious passive breaths? The parallel between Fuguet's McOndo and the socioeconomic model imposed on Chile under the autocratic rule of Augusto Pinochet (and under the pseudodemocracy that followed) is so close as to be stifling. No wonder Fuguet's celebrity-obsessed and consumer-minded virtuality is so close to the ready-for-export image that Chilean politicians and investment-hungry businessmen have been promoting for the last thirty years. Add a smidgen of alternative cool—just the thing to prove your middle-class credentials—and you've got exact Chilean replicas of sated, rebellious, hyper-hip American suburban youth. All you're missing are sundries like real celebrities, a movie industry, local music scenes, and enough kids with piercings.

In this respect, Alberto Fuguet's work turns out to be fictional in more than the obvious sense. A short spin around Santiago reveals the absolute absence of an infrastructure of hip, the sort of thing detailed by Ellis in Los Angeles or Tama Janowitz in New York. After nine years of crowing about having joined the ranks of First World economies, Chile's capital boasts few if any world class restaurants, a single six-mile stretch of highway on which to drag the Jeeps and Blazers Fuguet repeatedly mentions, and a nightlife still stunted from the effects of seventeen long years of curfews under military rule. The urbane, overdrawn vision of Santiago Fuguet presents, from his early short story collection *Sobredosis* ("Overdose") to the 1997 English-language edition of *Mala Onda* published by St. Martin's Press, is to the reality of Third World Chile as Internet sex is to physical coitus: a pale, desperate and unimaginative rendition of the real thing.

Even Matias Vicuña, the protagonist of *Mala Onda*, Fuguet's novel-length crib of *Less Than Zero,* seems to agree. In one passage Matias achieves an almost Joycean epiphany from an observation of Chilean fast food so inane that it deserves to be quoted in toto: "Pumper Nic is full, like it is every Saturday. The smell of french fries, of grease, engulfs me. I like it. It's the smell of the United States, I think. The smell of progress. It makes me think of Orlando and Disney World, of Miami, of McDonald's and Burger King and Kentucky Fried Chicken and Carl's Jr and Jack-in-the-Box. Pumper Nic—even the name sounds pathetic to me, way too Third World. It isn't all that bad, but it's a bad copy, that's the thing. It's not authentic."

Besides being an underdeveloped "Pumper Nic" copy of American literary fast food, *Mala Onda* is a shameless artifact of the culture it coyly pretends to criticize—as innately radical as a Rage Against the Machine album with Che Guevara's mug on the cover or a car commercial blaring a Jimi Hendrix guitar solo. Small wonder then that a book like *Mala Onda*—a novel set ostensibly in the Ellis-blessed golden age of the early Eighties but firmly steeped in Nineties globalism—appeals to a readership that normally does not buy novels. Its real message is a marketing triumph, a Hispanic repackaging of America's melding of consumption and cool. Fuguet's vision is a simple one: *¡El quiere su MTV!* His beef is aptly summarized by Nacho, one of Matias's spoiled friends in *Mala Onda.* "When," he demands in the nasal tones of that dude Hamlet, "are they going to start playing the Ramones or the Sex Pistols here?"

Nowhere in *Mala Onda* do the full third of Chileans living in poverty appear; rarely is there a sign of the country's rigid class stratification (the arrangement that makes Fuguet's comfortably apolitical life possible); never are we asked to wonder about the baroque social and cultural layering here that renders the span between the centuries a casual matter of strolling past a horse-drawn cart on the way to the corner video store. No, Fuguet and Co. know it is the duty of art to grace the halls of capital, to prove their country's bona fides as reliable consumers of global entertainment product. Or in Fuguet's words, "Pure virtual realism, pure McOndo literature"—an unfiltered reflection of "television, radio, the Internet, and movies which [McOndo writers] send back through [their] fiction."

Rather than "apolitical," perhaps the appropriate term for McOndo is "boosterism." Revel though it may in daring departures like drug use, sexual experimentation, and the inevitable outraged authority figures, one can't help but think that this is a literature of national salesmanship as surely as "magical realism" has become contrived exoticism for PC Americans. Consider the lengths to which McOndo goes to establish that the Latin cities it describes are in every way the equal of the Northern cities whose pleasures were sung by Ellis, Janowitz, and McInerney. Consider the ways in which its tales of profligate consumption and lifestyle rebellion serve curiously to emphasize the absolute up-to-dateness of the pleasures available to the various conspicuous consumers of Santiago or Lima or Madrid. McOndo reassures us that despite fresh memories of military regimes, these cities suffer no shortage of rule-breaking, hierarchy-questioning junior executive material. In addition to all that, McOndo puts to rest that most gnawing First World fear of all—that we might someday have to do business with people who don't share our tastes, know our TV references, and worship our brands. Perhaps it can do for Santiago what Sub Pop did for Seattle.

Hey, *señor*! Want fries or a shake to go with that book?

McSploitation

JIM ARNDORFER

UDDLED in Chicago's neon-scarred River North tourist district, Fadò Irish Pub desperately strains to pass for one of those quaint public houses common to postcards from the Old Sod. Its brightly painted façade, Celtic-lettered signage, and gimcrack-cluttered windows practically creak from the effort to project authenticity. The doorman who checks IDs typically has a brogue. All for naught, alas. None of these cosmetic touches can hide the fact Fadò stands three stories tall, a height completely unbecoming for a humble Irish pub. Such bulk is more in the league of Fadò's neighbors the Hard Rock Cafe, Planet Hollywood and Rainforest Cafe.

Fadò—Gaelic for "long ago" and pronounced F'doe—is the history of Ireland as Disney would "imagineer" it: the past as a preindustrial idyll full of familiar, entertaining, and edifying scenery—with anything that might offend or trouble painstakingly excised. There are no paintings of Cromwell's butchery at Drogheda or reenactments of the Great Potato Famine here; indeed nothing in Fadò explicitly indicates that for eight centuries Éire was occupied and often

brutally exploited by the hated Saxon. None of that bummer blarney! The prime mover behind the bar is Guinness Brewing—which is in fact a British company, part of the London-based conglomerate Diageo, which also owns Burger King, Pillsbury, and United Distillers & Vintners—so it probably sees little advantage in exhuming such unpleasant facts. Fadò would rather plunder the breadth of Irish history, from the Stone Age through the early twentieth century, to fabricate a pastiche past in which lighthearted bogtrotters worked hard, prayed hard, drank hard, sang songs, and bought quaint things with nary a grumble about their lot.

The past-as-playground rendition of Irish history unfolds as soon as you step inside. At the entrance a fake dolmen—a table-like megalith prehistoric Irelanders would raise for the honored dead—towers over you. From there the ground level is split into three rooms supposedly representative of different eras in Irish history. First up is the Gaelic pub. Here you're to sip your pint, meditate on the murals decorating the light wood walls and reach spiritual communion with the

fun-loving Goidelic Celts who conquered Ireland around 500 B.C.
and sang beautiful ballads when
they weren't seizing slaves. A row
of semi-secluded wooden tables,
calculatedly rough-hewn, clings to
the east wall.

Moving on, customers enter the
stone-walled Cottage Industries
pub, which absurdly celebrates the
subsistence economy of nineteenth
century rural Ireland. To commemo-
rate that era of famine and want,
Fadò has decorated the room with
the now-quaint workaday imple-
ments of an economy that broke
backs and drove hundreds of thousands to board ships for the peril-
ous passage to Amerikay. A loom
hangs from the ceiling; elsewhere
can be found a spinning wheel, a
butter churn, a wash stand, farm
tools, seed bags, and a collection of
buckets and bottles.

A weathered "currach"—the din-
ghy-like fishing boat still used in the
west of Ireland (at least when there
are tourists about)—hangs over the
stairwell leading to the "Land of
Saints and Scholars" mezzanine. This
space is modeled after the ship in
which St. Brendan allegedly sailed to
America during the sixth century; a
mural of a sea monster rending
Brendan's vessel is splashed across
the ceiling. Off to one side a seven-
foot-high Celtic cross stands on an
altar table. Painted icons of Saints
Brendan, Columcille, and Finian
stare out from the walls. It's like
drinking in church.

The north end of the third story is
devoted to the "Dublin Victorian Pub,"
which celebrates the queen whose
reign saw the Great Famine, two

crushed insurrections, and the "dyna-
mite campaign" in England—with
luxurious dark woods, velvet curtains,
and beveled glass. The area is dominated by a hundred-year-old, forty-
piece bar shipped over from Ireland.
Off to the sides are "snugs," the intimate booths favored by Irish characters and conspirators alike. A formidable collection of antique barrel taps
hangs on the east wall.

Mixed with a few pints, these
surroundings are intended to create
what the Irish—and especially the
marketers of Irishness—call *craic*
(pronounced "crack"), a Gaelic word
for a convivial atmosphere. Unfortunately, conversation is usually impossible because the sound system
is unbearably loud, recycling the
same tired hit-list of every pop sensation with even the faintest ties to
Erin. Gaelicity assaults from all
sides, making cogitation of any sort
a futile endeavor. But the politicos,
traveling businessmen, and young
executives who jam the place don't
seem to mind; they simply jostle and
holler as if they were in a sports bar.

People choose to visit Fadò for the
same reason they go to its theme-
restaurant neighbors: They want to
be immersed in an entertaining fantasy. The Rock and the Planet provide an escape into the world of celebrity; the Rainforest indulges a
fashionable consumerist eco-poli-
tics; Fadò offers a portal into white
exoticism. It's a fantasy Chicago has
always done well. Consider the
blues bar, long a fixture on Chicago's
must-do tourist circuit and a virtual
emporium of the exotic, even though
you're more likely to share your
table with a howling fratboy or

glassy-eyed management consultant than a hard-bitten migrant from the Delta. A place like Fadò, on the other hand, affords the white American thrill-seeker an opportunity to wallow in maudlin sentimentality and exult in the illicit passions of a subaltern minority without embarrassing reminders of his own place in history—that is to say, without thinking about race. Ireland and Irishness fit such a need perfectly. Not only for the more than forty million Americans who claim at least a wee bit of Irish blood, but for Celtophiles who see the Emerald Isle and its people as embodiments of old-fashioned clannishness and underdog pluck.

Irishness certainly is a desirable commodity. Once content to be Irish only on St. Patrick's Day, with all its antics, speechifying, and moronic uses of the color green, Americans—white ones, anyway—now demand more high-minded representations of the Gael. The culture industry has obliged. Michael Flatley has danced, live and on video with prerecorded taps, into the hearts of millions in the bombastic "Lord of the Dance." The New Age Celtic strains of the various *Titanic* soundtracks have served as background music for dinner parties coast to coast. Audiences have adored Edward Burns as the sexy bohemian with a heart of family values in *The Brothers McMullen*, and cried along with Matt Damon's sexy, two-fisted supergenius in *Good Will Hunting*. Frank McCourt's memoir of hunger in New York and Ireland, *Angela's Ashes*, won a Pulitzer and prompted an ill-considered second act by his brother Malachy. More is on the way: A sequel to *Angela's Ashes* and a film treatment are in the works.

Marie Antoinette and her attendants played at being peasants; bored nineteenth century English gentlemen idealized the sensuousness of Italy; Irishness sells to Americans because it represents authenticity and tradition in an often depressingly transient and hollow culture. Religion and faith are untroubled parts of "Irish" lives. Family bonds are strong. Neighbors know and help each other. Work is valued but so is play. Song and dance are in their blood—you saw how those paddies got down in the *Titanic*'s steerage! Good conversation and a sly, authority-tweaking humor spring naturally from their lips. This perception is nothing new: It was part of the vision of nineteenth

Grating to the Oldies

Excerpts from "Ed Debevic's Costume and Character Guide."

At Ed Debevic's we're proud to say that we were one of the first restaurants to incorporate our special brand of entertainment into the dining experience. Since we opened our first restaurant in Phoenix, Arizona in 1984, many other restaurants have come along to offer things like the opportunity to see (but not to touch) various artifacts used in Hollywood motion pictures, the chance to dine in an artificial rain forest, and some will offer a glimpse at a guitar once used by a legend of rock music.

Although these are all interesting, we offer something that they do not. Ed Debevic's is **Live** entertainment. Our customers have come to know us by such names as "the place where the servers dance on the counter" or "the place with the funny waitresses." It is the incorporation of these elements that has made Ed's successful and will ensure our success into the twenty first century. Being chosen as a cast member at Ed Debevic's means that we believe that you have the ability to be an important part of our continued success.

[T]he wait staff at Ed's is a breed apart. Clad in vintage clothing and costumes, they look and act the part of greasers, nerds, housewives and mechanics, just to mention a few.

As you read this manual, you will find ideas that you can use to build your own, special character from the ground up. If you find that you need some help, don't hesitate to talk to your General Manager or to me, the Entertainment Director. After all, that's what we're here for...

[A]s front of the house employees at Ed Debevic's, we are the source of entertainment for our guests. If a joke is made, it should be on us (or rather, our characters). We should never put a guest in the position of being a source of entertainment for us or for the other guests.

As a cast member it is essential that you remember the reason you're here. In a performance space like ours, the audience is all around you. They aren't just at the tables in your section but in the tables throughout the restaurant as well as those who are waiting to be seated. We want every one of our guests leaving feeling as though they have "experienced" Ed Debevic's. That is your job. Share the experience.

When interacting with guests and Ed Debevic's, your challenge is to make sure that your character becomes part of the punch line of an elaborate, ongoing joke. A greaser, for example, is known for being a tough guy and not so much for his cerebral prowess. What if your character was a greaser who realized that he wasn't very smart and because of this continually misused big, impressive words in an attempt to cover it up. Another example would be a tired, housewife character who accessorizes her housecoat and dons elaborate makeup in an attempt to appear more glamorous.

Stock Characters
The Greaser (Rebel)

The greaser personality is one of overcompensation. He overcompensates for his lack of book smarts and social skills with an overdeveloped attitude and physique. For the greaser, the most important thing is being "cool." The way he walks and talks reflect this emphasis. His movements are slow and contemplative and his walk looks more like a glide. A short fuse is the trademark of the classic greaser but you'll never hear him raise his voice.

Clad in black leather and jeans, the greaser is always ready for battle. That's how he takes his life... one fight at time. The only problem is that he rarely knows what he's fighting for. His wallet has a chain that hooks to his belt loop and he always has a fresh pack of Lucky Strike smokes rolled in the sleeve of his black t-shirt.

Although he is tough, he does have a sensitive side. Perhaps this is part of the reason he maintains such a "thick skin." On occasion, this "softer side" shows through especially around children or animals. It is the unconditional acceptance that only they can offer that he appreciates.

The important thing to remember about our greaser is that he has a past. He probably spent his formative years seeking the acceptance and approval of others. Failing to do so, he has decided to keep people at a distance and maintain a "I'm O.K. no matter what you think" way of thinking. No matter what, his hair is always perfect. Piled high in a pompadore [sic] and secured with gobs of butch wax or hair tonic giving him the infamous reputation of "greaser," a name born from the oily appearance of his hair.

century Irish romantic nationalism and has been propagated ever since by the entertainment industry and the Irish Tourist Board. Only nowadays, deep-pocketed marketers have the latest in demographic marketing tools and segmentation strategies to cram this vision down our throats.

The accepted narrative of the Irish experience in America also bolsters the ideological foundation of the increasingly conservative body politic. In the New World the Irish contended with bigotry and slaved at menial jobs, but by dint of hard work overcame all obstacles and assimilated into the respectable life of the suburbs and office cubicles. This myth of Irish advancement omits such important factors as political cronyism, the munificence of the New Deal, and the expansion of government, but it does promote self-satisfaction among white folks. If they could make it, the thinking goes, so can anyone. Unspoken but always understood is the contrast of the Irish narrative with that of the other major, if more threatening, exotic group in the United States: African-Americans. The historic travails of the two groups are often compared, and audiences everywhere nodded when a character in the 1991 film *The Commitments*, which told the story of an aspiring Dublin soul band, announced that the Irish were "the blacks of Europe." Of course, at some point the Irish in America "became white," in the words of Noel Ignatiev, but that doesn't figure in the story *craic* peddlers want to tell.

II.

BENEATH its folksy Hibernian veneer, Fadò is a cog in a global marketing strategy engineered by Guinness Brewing. Looking to boost sales of its renowned stout, the brewer has orchestrated an alliance of designers, developers, investors and marketers in the mass production of a supposedly quintessential Irish institution: the pub.

In the late Eighties, Guinness noticed that Irish investors were making a killing with home-style pubs in France and Germany. Hungry to build its international market share, the brewer decided to get a piece of the Irish pub's new international vogue and create just the right atmosphere to coax skeptical foreign customers, Italian and

Estonian alike, to ramp up their consumption of the strange black liquid. Guinness gave a name to its globe-spanning sales strategy: the Irish Pub Concept.

Guinness then started rounding up accomplices. It tapped chefs to design menus, hired recruiters to find appropriately accented bar staff, and commissioned the Irish Pub Company—a newly created subsidiary of Dublin-based McNally Design Group, an international planner and builder of restaurants, hotels, bowling alleys, and discos—to create cookie-cutter pub patterns. Irish Pub architects and researchers spent months visiting hundreds of pubs in Ireland, analyzing and cataloging such minutiae as joinery details and floor finishes, all to quantify the essence of an Irish pub.

Reasoning that it didn't make sense to get its hands dirty in the bar business, Guinness began searching for outside investors and developers. Working with Irish Pub, the brewer began pitching the idea to venture capitalists in Europe and beyond. Before long pubs started springing up in Europe, the Middle East and Asia, in cities from Dublin to Hong Kong.

Guinness and its partners waited until 1995 before casting a cold eye across the western ocean to the world's largest beer market, the United States. Putting out feelers, Irish Pub initially encountered skepticism, partly because Irish bars had a bad rap in the States, where they're often seen either as cheesy fratboy hangouts or nondescript dives that drew illegal immigrants and IRA supporters. In fact, Irish Pub had to put up money for a showcase pub before it finally struck a deal with a group of Irish and American investors called Fadò Irish Pub Company. The first bar—named Fadò—opened in Atlanta in January 1996 and before long became one of the country's leading draft sales outlets for Guinness stout and Harp lager. The other investors soon bought out Irish Pub Company's stake in the bar.

The designer chose Atlanta as its first site to demonstrate that a city doesn't need a large Irish population to support its establishments. Irish culture had a strong appeal among young professionals, tourists, and conventioneers of all backgrounds, and the Atlanta bar proved it. Encouraged by the Atlanta bar's success, investors have since opened twenty bars in the United States designed by Irish Pub. Fadò Irish Pub itself has gone on to open eponymous establishments in Austin,

Our greaser goes by the name of Spike, but some guys he runs with are named Jake, Snake, Vinny, Rocco, Blade, and Bulldog.

Please note: "Greaser Chicks" are also acceptable characters.

Born to be a Waitress (The Career Girl)

Balancing six burgers on her left arm and four baskets of fries on her right, this gal glides down the aisle without losing a pickle. She's quick, she's bright and she loves to talk. Just one lunch in her section and you'll feel as though you've known her for years. She'll make you feel right at home when she says "Get your elbows off the table" or "People all over the world don't have enough to eat and you can't clean your plate."

Crisp and fresh in her starched uniform, you can tell by the way she looks that she takes her job seriously. She keeps a fancy hanky pinned in place with her name tag and her apron is always secured in back with a double bow. She is truly the model waitress. In addition to a flawless appearance, she can take an order, snap her gum, and wipe down a table, all at the same time.

Our career girl has a particular take on life, not to mention a sense of humor, that only many years of waiting on people can give a person. Talk about your customer complaints, well, she's heard them all from cold food to cold service. She has worked in more diners, in more states, than she cares to remember but she still wouldn't trade her job for a chance to meet Elvis.

She may seem a bit "hard-nosed" at times but that nose is always to the grindstone and her mind's on business because, as she puts it: "I got a stack of bills at home that aren't about to pay themselves. Until they do, you'll find me right here, six days a week doin' what I do best."

In addition to her uniform and fancy hanky, our career girl wears a waitress's tiara and comfortable (very clean) shoes. She accessorizes her ensemble with items that reflect her personality (pins, buttons, etc.).

Our career girl goes by the name of Mabel, but she has worked with girls that go by names like Gladys, Edna, Midge, Madge, Ruby, and Marge.

The Tired Housewife

It's 5:30 A.M. when the alarm shatters the silence. "I'm awake," she mumbles as she nudges her snoring husband, shuts off the alarm and stumbles to the kitchen, where she puts on a pot of dangerously strong coffee.

As she sips her first cup of the day, she runs down the list of errands that she must get done before she goes to work. Do the laundry, pay bills, go to the bank, drive the kids to school, and make sure that her husband isn't

Texas; Washington, D.C.; Seattle; and Cleveland. The Chicago bar opened its doors in November 1997. Guinness claims it has opened more than fourteen hundred Irish Pub Concept bars around the world.

Nevertheless, sales growth of Guinness stout has lagged behind that of other global brands, and the brewer now pins its hopes on expanding its market share in the United States. Irish Pub Concept establishments figure to be a significant part of Guinness's marketing effort. The brewer envisions about four hundred such bars opening in major and smaller cities; Irish Pub alone hopes to open a hundred establishments in the United States over the next five years and it continues to hunt for new partners.

As novel as the Irish Pub Concept may seem, it follows in the footsteps of a recent and rather unfortunate cultural phenomenon: the theme restaurant, two or three of which seem to occupy every block in River North, thanks to the tireless "vision" of Chicago entrepreneur Rich Melman. Melman got his start in the early Seventies, one of a few savvy restaurateurs who recognized that, in a culture saturated by the entertainment industry and electronic media, there was money to be made by injecting elements of theater and carnival into "the dining experience." He opened his first establishment, R. J. Grunt's, in 1971. Grunt's offered an offbeat, casual vibe with its hanging plants, modern art, and that definitive gustatory innovation of the decade: the salad bar. Catering to the groovy young singles then gentrifying the Lincoln Park neighborhood, the place was a hit.

Thirty years ago restaurants typically needed only to be clean and

serve decent food to make a buck. Now it's difficult to find a restaurant not animated by an entertainment concept. While it's true that some of the high-end theme chains—Fashion Cafe and the Rainforest Cafe, for example—have hit a wall (mostly because they served lousy food), entertainment still has become a standard of the eatery industry in the post-Melman universe. When people step into a restaurant, they now expect to enter a different world. Sometimes, of course, that world is one better left in the dustbin of history, as in the case of the popular Chicago restaurant Le Colonial, which sumptuously evokes the languid, sensuous milieu of French Indochina in the Twenties, with bamboo fittings, lazy ceiling fans, and sepia-tinted photographs of peasants carrying water, harvesting rice, and hefting a sweating, porcine worthy in a sedan chair. The pictures, one gathers, are the next best thing to staffing the joint with real peons. The self-impressed patrons of Le Colonial would hardly be likely to endorse the viciousness of the French regime in Indochina, and yet the nostalgia for an era of entitlement, deference, and abject servitude dovetails nicely with the leitmotifs of our own time: the polarization of rich and poor, the no-excess-is-too-absurd imperative to please that is imposed on service industry employees.

At Fadò, the staff plays along gamely in the bar's exaggerated effort to convince its customers that they are experiencing something other than a denatured spectacle called into being by transnational investors. They proudly boast how the chairs you sit on, the bar you lean on, and the floors you tread upon all were made in Ireland. The patrons by and large appear to love the contrivance of the bar, and the air is abuzz with them excitedly telling the story of Fadò to friends who are experiencing the *craic* for the first time. No one really seems to mind, or even acknowledge, the irony that the quaint Irish pub they are drinking in is a very modern creation brought into being by the sort of large conglomerates that are destroying local institutions ranging from the drug store to the butcher shop. Everyone's too enthralled with the "authenticity" of the Made in Ireland surroundings and the fun of playing at Irishness; on every visit to Fadò I have either heard someone ape a brogue or seen someone break into a half-assed jig.

late for work again this week. When does it all end?

Well, her husband gets to work on time and kids are all at school. Now it's time for her to get to the diner because she has to be able to cover the check she just wrote for the water bill. Needless to say, there's no time for makeup, and she'll have to wait until she gets to work to take her curlers out of her hair so a scarf will have to do for now. As she gets into the car, she realizes that she's still wearing her housecoat. There's no time to change now, so it's off to work, curlers, housecoat and all.

On her way to the diner, traffic is much worse than usual, and she ends up getting there a few minutes late. There's no time now to take those curlers out so she decides to hit the floor and start waitin' tables. When her day ends here, she'll head on home and start cooking dinner for her husband and five kids.

Our poor, tired housewife follows the same routine every day. Just imagine how she must feel. Despite her near exhaustion, she finds a smile for everyone and a pleasant "hello."

Our tired housewife goes by the name of Eunice, but other women on her block are named Helen, Beatrice, Fanny, Alice, and Norma.

The Beauty School Dropout

It's not hard to spot this beauty queen. She's the one who applies everything she ever learned at beauty school, to herself, every day (not to mention every cosmetic she ever bought). As far as the hair goes, the bigger the better. Just rat it and spray it. Her eyelashes are long, thick, black, and fake. The only boundaries her eye shadow knows are her eyebrows. Speaking of eye shadow, don't stop with one color, or matching colors for that matter. Just mix and match.

Despite her ridiculous appearance (never say that to her face) she considers herself the authority when it comes to cosmetic self-improvement. She has a hundred ideas for hairdos and just as many for makeup and nails. She'll never hesitate to lay then on ya. But whatever you do, don't take her up on her beauty advice. Before you can blink, she'll pull out the tools of the trade. They're never far away. She'll start clipping and curling, spraying and dying and when the hair spray settles, you'll look just like her. How fabulous!

This girl is always ready to go to work. She wears her pants skin tight with a pink lab coat (who knows, one day it may be a science) and white socks with Keds. She usually accessorizes her lab coat with a first-name initial pin, or her entire first name spelled out in rhinestones. Her makeup is **thick**.

Our beauty school drop-out goes by the name of Babs, but some of the girls in her coloring class are named Dolly, Frenchie, DeeDee, Flo, Pinky, and Maybelline.

Where's the harm in that? Hasn't Ireland been inundated for decades by millions upon millions of Americans searching for their roots, for the Blarney Stone, for the Book of Kells, for 7 Eccles Street? Millions of long-lost and annoying cousins, boring you with stories about their granny from Kerry and trying out their Hollywood brogues and donning their Aran sweaters and tweed flatcaps. And spending billions of dollars. Moreover, isn't the "Celtic Tiger," Ireland's vaunted high-tech and service-economy boom, the tourist trade writ digital?

Ironically, one gets a sense of the real Ireland's predicament in Fadò's recreation of post office/grocery/bar supposedly typical of rural Ireland. A telephone switchboard is set in a corner, and stacked on the shelves are boxes of Jacobs cream crackers and Oxo cubes, bags of Mosse's brown bread mix, and jars of Fruitfield marmalade. Adverts for Players cigarettes, Marsh Co.'s biscuits and Wills's Cut Gold Bar tobacco hang on the walls. The whole room effectively breaks Ireland down into brand names. It's the way America understands the world these days.

I once saw behind the majestic Victorian mahogany bar two bartenders arguing—Arguing! How wonderfully Irish!—over which artifacts in the pub were authentic antiques and which ones were newly minted and artificially aged impostors. The debate lasted for some time with neither side yielding—another indubitably Irish characteristic. But the disagreement raised a new question: Is Ireland the country doomed forever to live in the shadow of Ireland the brand?

I'm OK, Eeyore OK

Johnny Payne

IT was a beautiful day in the Hundred-Acre Planned Community. The sun was shining on the green grass where all of the houses backed up onto the nine-hole golf course. Christopher Robin had come out at dawn to get in a couple of early rounds, for, as he had often been told by Owl, the early bird catches the worm. He was under par, and so his disposition was cheery.

Pretty soon, along came Pooh. "Hello, Christopher Robin."

"Hello, Pooh."

"Christopher Robin, have you seen my Honey? I've been looking everywhere for my Honey."

"No, Pooh. She hasn't been round this morning. How about a quick six or seven holes? Be a good bear, and fetch me my driver out of the bag."

"Oh, dear, oh, dear. This is just terrible," remarked Pooh. "She and I had a tiff last evening, Christopher Robin. My obsessive-compulsive disorder is getting out of hand, I fear. I keep feeling like my fingers are sticky. Every time afterward, you know, I keep getting up to wash my hands and mouth. To get the Honey off, you see. But no matter how much I wash, they still feel sticky and dirty."

Christopher teed off, leaving a small divot in the sod, which he carefully replaced. "Go see Owl, Silly Old Bear. He's better than Masters and Johnson. A chat with him and you'll be right as rain."

"Oh, bother," said Pooh. "Oh, hot and bother. I can't afford him just now. My annual quota of visits ran out on my insurance. Are you sure my Honey isn't at your place?"

"Listen here," replied Christopher, taking slight umbrage. "Who do you take me for? Rabbit?"

"Goodness me, Christopher, I didn't mean to imply anything."

"That's all right, Dear Bear. I dare say it wouldn't hurt for that sort of rumor about me to make the rounds. As much time as I spend alone with you, some of the neighbors are starting to gossip that I'm a hom—a homos—"

Right then Tigger, the newest addition to the Hundred-Acre Planned Community, came racing through, knocking Pooh straightaway off his feet. His hearing was keen, and he didn't want to miss out on any juicy details about his new neighbors.

"Homonym?" he guessed. "Homunculus? Homogeneous? Homeostasis?"

"One of those, I suppose," sighed Christopher Robin. "Some big word or other. But it didn't have a very pleasant sound."

"Tiggers like big words," cried Tigger, and dashed off as quick as lightning, shouting "Mendacity! Mendacity!" in a voice like hot buttered rum.

Not long after, Kanga came hopping by, all in spandex and with an empty snuggli. She had dropped Roo at a good, church-based pre-school program emphasizing structured play, and was on her way to a rendezvous with the passionate, virile groundskeeper of the Hundred-Acre Planned Community. She was a twentysomething, while her most recent husband was an arid, icy, lifeless, impotent fortysomething and very rich City Planner, who spent his days bitterly plotting the destruction of forests to make way for nine-hole golf courses and suburban homes. Kanga no longer loved him, but she did like driving a shiny new sport utility vehicle to her appointments with Owl. And she was grateful for having the money to relocate to a white-flight community where she didn't have to worry her pony-tailed head about school redistricting or quotas.

"Robin. Pooh," she greeted them aloofly.

"Hello, Kanga," they both said at once.

"I see you've met our new neighbor," she observed. "What good is a security gate? I knew it was only a matter of time before Tiggers started moving in and driving the property values down."

"I believe the proper term is *Tegro*," Christopher carefully and patiently corrected her.

"Tigger, Tegro, what's the difference?" she replied irritably. "If you listen to them talk, they call each other Tigger all the time. And no one takes offense. Why can't I say it too?"

"I'm not sure," Pooh mused tentatively. "But I do believe it means Something Different if another species uses the word in describing a species not its own. Have you seen my Honey, Kanga?"

"No, I haven't, Pooh. But if you run across mine, would you tell him I'm at Mother's Day Out. See you in the funny papers." And she went on her merry way.

"Is she really going into the funny papers, Christopher Robin?"

"I think that's what they call a figure of speech, Pooh."

"What's a figure of speech, Christopher Robin?"

"Oh, Pooh, you're ever the ingénue, aren't you?" replied Christopher Robin, and gave him a big hug, though not too big of one, lest the mini-blinds of the houses adjoining the nine-hole golf course be quizzically lifted. "Listen, Dear Bear. I see Eeyore coming over the hill. We need to do Something about him. He's having even worse problems than yourself."

"How so?"

"Owl says he's in 'a mild to moderate clinical depression.' Eeyore is so negative about everything, and did you ever notice that his affect seems flat?"

"Should it be round, then, Christopher Robin?"

"Something like that, Dear Fuzzy

Ursa Minor. Owl says Eeyore needs to be medicated in the worst way. Let's see if we can cheer him up."

Just about then, Eeyore arrived on the fairway, and gloomily looked about, as if he didn't quite know where he had landed.

"Hello, Eeyore," Pooh said brightly, in his Most Welcoming Voice. Yet he couldn't help adding, a bit whinily, "Have you seen my Honey, Eeyore?"

"I have of late, but wherefore I know not, lost all my mirth," rejoindered Eeyore. "This goodly frame the earth seems to me a sterile promontory."

"It's not sterile, Eeyore. It's fecu—fecu—it's all green and growy, Dear Little Hoofed Mammal," said Christopher Robin.

"It may look that way to you," replied Eeyore, "but what do you make of all those Lawn Application flags I keep tripping over. The grass doesn't really grow this green all by itself, Christopher. That groundskeeper creeps in here under cover of night, after his trysts with Kanga, and spreads chemical fertilizers. That stuff burns the turf, you know. You should try grazing in it. Then you'd have heartburn, just like me."

"It's all a matter of perspective," Christopher pressed on, determinedly. "To be frank with you, Eeyore, Owl says he's tried to put you on those no-feeling-sad-pills, and according to him, you refuse to take them. He said they were tricic—tricic—"

Tigger came roaring through, bowling Eeyore over, so that the Melancholy Donkey ended sitting clean upside down. Tigger bounded into the nearest tree limb. "Tricycles? Triceratops? Trichinosis?"

"Something like that," said Christopher.

"They're called tricyclics," moaned Eeyore. "And I did try them. All I got for my trouble was skin rashes, blurred vision, and alopetia."

"What's alopetia?" inquired Pooh. "Is it something to eat?"

"It means hair loss. Sort of like my prematurely receding hairline, Pooh," explained Christopher Robin. "Runs in my family, along with the Hapsburg Lip. It doesn't bother me a whit."

"Easy for you to say," complained Eeyore from his upside-down position. "But hair loss is devastating to a donkey. My fur is my only good feature. Anyway, tricyclics make you lose—well, Something Else Important."

"I know," said Christopher. "Your libi—libi—"

"Liberty?" quizzed Tigger. "Libations? Liberace?"

"And excuse me for saying this, Eeyore," continued Christopher. "But how can you lose something you never had to begin with?"

"I may not have much," muttered Eeyore. "But in the land of the blind, the one-eyed man is king."

"Now, now," calmed Christopher. "No sense getting your feathers ruffled, Dear Beast of Burden. All in the world I was leading up to was suggesting that you try Prozac. It doesn't have any of those nasty side-effects that the other no-feeling-sad-pills do. Well, it does mildly suppress your libi—libi—your Appetite. But that isn't such a bad thing. In fact, if those of us who live in the Hundred-Acre Planned Community have any problem, it's too much Appetite. We'd be better off without it, I think. All Appetite leads to in the end is unfriendly feelings."

"Hmm," reflected Eeyore. "I wouldn't mind trying this Prozac you speak of. But I hate being the only one. I already feel like enough of a misfit as it is."

"Misfit?" Christopher laughed merrily. "If you tallied up the property lines of all the people around here on Prozac, you'd use up at least Seventy-Five of the Hundred Acres. Pooh's been on it, and Kanga's on megadoses right now. Rabbit's on it as well, not because he's sad exactly, but to help control his Appetite. He has the biggest Appetite of anyone I know. Owl even prescribes it for himself. And he's so wise and everything."

"What about you, Christopher?" asked Eeyore imploringly. "Are you the only one of us who doesn't need it? Is it because you are a human and we are animals?"

"Are you kidding?" replied Christopher Robin. "Why do you think I'm smiling all the confounded time? Have you ever once seen me in recent times that I didn't have a smile on my face? Ever since I started on that pill, I've been Wonderfully Happy."

"True," admitted Eeyore. "Very true."

So Eeyore agreed to take Prozac, and it was only then that he truly became one of the Friends. They all played golf together that very afternoon, to celebrate Eeyore's Great Decision. Christopher Robin was three over par, but he sauntered off whistling anyway.

THE BAFFLER Lit-Buddy

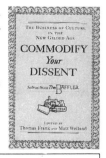

The Penalty of Leadership

Cadillac and Class Consciousness

STEPHEN DUNCOMBE

*The 1959 Cadillac speaks so eloquently—in so many ways—of the man who sits at its wheel
. . . . This magnificent 1959 Cadillac will tell this wonderful story about you.*

—Advertisement, 1959 Cadillac

ESCAPE is our national narrative, and automobiles are the twentieth century's vehicle for this fantasy: a way to flee the farm, the city, adolescence, middle age, frustration, poverty, class, other people, yourself. Just drive. But cars are more than just a means of escape, they're also projections of who we'll be when we arrive. Automobiles are the dream life of America, the tools with which we write our autobiographies. If in the first decades of this century the working classes glimpsed freedom in a Ford, the middle classes, stuck with their Fords, saw their aspirations drive up in a Cadillac. To know the great middle, therefore, you must study the Caddy.

"The Penalty of Leadership," announces the headline of an early Cadillac advertisement, one of the first to dispense entirely with any mention of utilitarian mechanics and rely instead upon the story it tells to sell the goods. Reading like a college sophomore's coffee-addled crib notes for next morning's exam on Kipling and Nietzsche, the 1915 ad describes, of all things, the "penalty" in store for the sober bourgeois who aspires to the level of the Cadillac:

> In every field of human endeavor, he that is first must perpetually live in the white light of publicity. Whether the leadership be vested in man or manufactured product, emulation and envy are ever at work.

In 1915, of course, business was not yet recognized as the holy calling it is now understood to be. The Progressive Era public demonized the businessman's greed, while intellectuals reviled him as a tasteless boob. Slings and arrows everywhere. But the ad boys were there to aid and comfort. No matter what others might think or say, you, the Cadillac-driving elect, are "geniuses" just like the inventor Fulton, the artist Whistler, and (surprise, surprise) the composer Wagner. The common cut of man, however, cannot hope to understand excellence:

> Failing to equal or excel, the follower seeks to depreciate and to destroy, but only confirms once more the superiority of that which he strives to supplant.

Oh, suffer those who deserve to reign. Dipping again into the tidal pool of Social Darwinism, the admen conclude:

> There is nothing new in this. It is as old as the world and as old as the human passions: envy, fear, greed, ambition and the desire to surpass. And it all avails to nothing. If the leader truly leads he remains—the leader. . . . That which deserves to live—Lives.

The writers cranking out copy for Cadillac had a good grasp of the pop philosophies of their day, but they also understood something far more enduring: the complexity of class and status in the United States. In this democratic land of Mammon, status is something you buy. No titles to defer to or impenetrable class hierarchies to hold you down, you can start a Ragged Dick and end up a John D. Rockefeller. But if you can get it you can always lose it. This is the double edge of class mobility. Like their Calvinist ancestors, the up-and-comers of the early twentieth century were continually looking for a sign that they were the chosen—that in the struggle for supremacy they deserved to live.

But it wasn't enough to assure yourself. In this war of all against all you had to convince others as well. You needed to show "the followers" (which at this moment, *sans* Cadillac, you were most assuredly in the ranks of) that you belonged at the top. The Cadillac was a visible sign of status, the updated market equivalent to the sumptuary laws of four centuries past that explicitly defined what clothes commoners could and could not wear. The European aristocrats who de-vised these laws did so while looking nervously over their shoulder at the rising bourgeoisie, passing silly edicts—no "Silke of purple color" for any but Earls and Knights of the Garter—as a last-ditch effort to hold on to their place in a world where divine rule and blood rite were being washed away by the tides of money and trade. They lost. Now the bourgeoisie, victors in that revolution, faced the same problem. In the great capitalist shakeup that allowed people to escape their lowly peasant origins, the new powers-that-be faced the constant dread that their place at the top was a temporary one.

And Cadillac felt their pain. The image the brand projected was less about keeping up with the Joneses and more about transcending the simple Joneses and their world entirely. "Envy, fear, greed, ambition, and the desire to surpass"; everything you now felt as a striving member of the middle class would be felt by someone else—by everyone else—but not by you, for behind the wheel of your Cad you would become an American aristocrat, outside of the class system altogether. It would be lonely at the top, yes, but this was the Penalty of Leadership.

For years Cadillac offered up variations on this theme of a transcendent American aristocracy. Selling a dream only possible in the New World, Cadillac's model names hearkened back to the Old World: Biarritz, Concours, Seville, La Salle, and de Ville brought to mind dukes and counts, castles and villas (the company itself was named for Antoine de la Mothe Cadillac, the minor Gascon noble who founded Detroit). Advertisements gave form to the car's aristocratic pretensions. Art directors in the Twenties frequently parked the Cadillac in front of those pseudo-Old World estates American robber barons were so fond of building. Or, failing that, they were placed in exotic and ultramodern locales like a Zeppelin aerodrome (unwittingly drawing associations between the Caddy and another species of transport that would soon fail the Darwinian test). Estate or aerodrome, Cadillacs were sold as the admission ticket to "Wherever the Admired and Notable Congregate."

As ruling class power migrated in the years after World War II from titans of industry to corporate CEOs, the dreams of the middle class, and the ads for Cadillac, followed suit. The new aristocrat was no longer a lone genius but a team player. "It is not at all unusual," an advertisement knowingly confides in 1955, "for a fine American corporation to have its entire board membership represented on the Cadillac owner list."

The postwar Cadillac owner was also a family man: A picture of wife and four kids lined up on a couch present "The World's Best Reason for Ordering a Cadillac." And he was a full-on consumer: No Cadillac ad from the mid-Fifties to the early Sixties was complete without some luxury product—a garish emerald necklace or gaudy diamond tiara—in-

congruously hovering above the automobile. Despite its domestication, the promise of privilege remained Cadillac's selling point. Another 1955 advertisement depicts an obsequious manservant opening the door for a couple stepping out of a Coupe de Ville, while the aspiring owner is reassured that, when he shows up in a Caddy, he will "find that he is accorded an extra measure of courtesy and respect." "Perhaps this will be the year," still another ad from that year promises— presumably when the executive might haul himself up and out of the rat race where he gets no respect.

But America was changing. The bourgeois dream of aristocratic escape that Cadillac had reliably supplied for decades was challenged by new stories, and Americans were exploring other ways of stepping off the treadmill. After the war, the middle classes moved to the suburbs and took out mortgages, mowed their lawns and bred babies, bought pop-up toasters and hydramatic cars, and generally set about enjoy-

ing the Good Life denied them throughout the Depression and the war. Something, however, was missing in the peace and quiet of suburbia: the drama and meaning of the last two difficult decades. A restless few returned from bombing runs over Europe to form the Hell's Angels, or never got past the disembarkment point from the Pacific Theater and made the scene in San Francisco. But the overwhelming masses of the postwar middle found their answer in the great consumer marketplace.

Cadillac did well for a time as a marketer of freedom and excitement. Cadillac, in fact, introduced nothing less than the tailfin, inspired by the Lockheed P-38 fighter plane, with its 1949 Fleetwood 60 Special. Elvis Presley did his part for the firm by ordering a 1955 model painted bright pink. The '59 model year was both the high point of this trajectory and also the beginning of the end. Extraordinary fins, with chromed, razor-sharp edges and rocket-styled tail lights erupted from the rear of that year's Caddy (and, later, from untold numbers of Hard Rock Cafe entrances, MTV videos, and anything else requiring an instant whiff of the "Fifties"). Ironically, though, the super-finned '59—possibly the division's most memorable car—was despised by Cadillac's core market, to whom it was a jukebox, exactly the wrong vehicular accouterment for a respectable executive on the move. (I've even been told that this most recognizable of Caddies is not included in the leather-bound, official History of Cadillac.) Cadillac could never deliver the fantasy of freedom in the way it had consistently provided the dream of dominance.

No, the Caddy was square. But therein lay its appeal. As social discontent spread to the sons and daughters of the great middle, Cadillac gave up its experiments with tailfins and became an island of calm. The kids might be smokin' a lid and makin' love-not-war in the back of a VW bus, but the men who ruled the country were barreling two-ton behemoths down the four-lane blacktop. Throughout the Sixties Cadillac was the car of the backlash, arrogantly holding to the privileges of aristocracy against the rising clamor for equality and justice. Their response to the War on Poverty was the "mink test," an experiment that proved that one's fur would be not be mussed by the auto's upholstery. Well into the Seventies and Eighties, Cadillac continued to sell the story of a ruling class that acted, and wanted to act, like a ruling class.

It was in this glorious, corpulent tradition that Cadillac made one last heaving push in the Nineties to restore their aristocratic "Standard of the World." Enter the bloatillac, obviously intended to look streamlined and prosperous at the same time, but in reality resembling nothing so much as an early Seventies Sedan de Ville with layers of blubber hung on the side. It is impossible to see one of these mid-Nineties bloatillacs creak by and not think of the standard editorial-page caricature of a "plutocrat": bulbous and waddling, a bag of money in one hand and a fat cigar in the other. Not coincidentally, the typical age of a Caddy owner today is sixty-five, rising, and thus, dying. And, as one of the weakest units of General Motors, so is Cadillac.

Cadillac has been dying for almost twenty years now. The division's sales peaked in 1978; they have been falling ever since. In the Eighties alone, sales of Sevilles and Eldorados fell by more than half. Even more damning are the immediate resale values of Cadillacs. (Cut loose from Detroit's sticker price and determined within a competitive market, resale values are the best indication of the real price and quality of an automobile.) In 1972, a good year for the Caddy, a Sedan de Ville driven off the lot retained 92 percent of its value. In 1975, a new Caddy kept only 83 percent, and by 1989 it was dropping a quarter. By 1997, 27 percent of the value of a new Sedan de Ville bloatillac leaked through the floorboards on the way home from the dealership. Compared to other domestic and foreign cars, the tragedy of Cadillac's resale value is even more sobering. The 1997 Sedan de Ville's depreciation is nearly double that of its Japanese luxury competitor, the Lexus LS (14 percent), and triple its economy cousin, the Chevy Malibu (9 percent). Throughout the Seventies and Eighties these low resale values meant that poor blacks looking for their slice of the good life—and later, déclassé white hipsters digging the kitsch irony of driving a Caddy-in-quotes—could snap up used Cadillacs for a song. As one might imagine, these new Caddy-driving populations did little to polish Cadillac's tarnished reputation as the car of the aristocracy.

II.

For all the puffery, Cadillac quality was once a tangible thing. The company pioneered electric ignition and air conditioning, and came out with a wonderfully monstrous V-16 engine in 1929. They built good cars. But for the past twenty years Cadillac has produced gas-guzzling boats that consistently receive bad ratings for quality, handling, and styling. And lest you think that things are changing in the total-quality Nineties: The sporty new 1998 Seville STS is reported by *The New York Times* to chatter at start-up, jerk at 30 mph, buzz at 45, and rattle at 65. Once you top 70, mysterious "out of sync movements" start thumping through

The New Myth of the Happy Worker

Brishen Rogers

In late 1990, the first Saturn rolled out of the Spring Hill, Tennessee plant that General Motors had been building, fine-tuning, and hyping for most of the Eighties. To announce the event, the ad agency for the GM division-that-could produced a TV commercial celebrating it as virtually the most important development in American culture and manufacturing since the Model T.

The spot features a Saturn "team member" (he would be known as a "worker" were he to toil in some less-empowering branch of the auto industry) with a subdued but distinct Detroit accent, every inch the noble, honest Midwestern worker. He says goodbye to his family, climbs into his baby-blue pickup, and leaves his farmhouse well before the Tennessee morning burns off last night's mist. This is the day, as a television on his kitchen table announces, when the first Saturn will roll off the line.

At his old job, this solid citizen tells us, he punched the clock but never really got the point. Nobody ever asked him what he thought. Then he heard about Saturn—a new company that takes workers' ideas into account—and liked what he heard. "Seems to me that when you see where your part fits into the big picture," he says, "it means a lot more."

Letting workers talk. It's such a damn fine all-American idea, it's surprising that nobody had thought of it before. And yet it was making waves. "We've got people watching us," he explains. "Some are for and some against. But I'll tell you, it's gonna be a great feeling to know that I was a small part of history." The spot closes with team members gazing at a new, gleaming white Saturn, and we grasp what's going on at Spring Hill: a new industrial idea, a new American mission of production, a project founded on the simple notion that it's good to let people talk.

In its brief history, Saturn Motors has won consumers' hearts with tales of workers finding fulfillment in Spring Hill. Saturn team members don't just slave away for wages, and they certainly don't fit the mold of the angry, alienated autoworker. By granting them and their union a voice in production decisions, the story goes, the Saturn plant has found a solution to the auto industry's fractious labor relations. Having received a voice, the story goes, workers at Saturn are happy, eccentric, even soulful. As they appear in more recent commercials, they are known to play cars like musical instruments; they dress like Social Distortion fans; they get to spend an afternoon painting instead of putting cars together. They're at peace with themselves and at one with the company.

In late February, those same workers tossed out the union leaders who'd been so close with GM management, replacing them with a more confrontational, less partnership-oriented team. This wasn't the first sign of dissent in Tennessee: Last summer, 96 percent of the autoworkers at the Spring Hill plant voted to authorize a strike, charging GM with scuttling any opportunity for real democracy. Saturn is not an oasis in an autocratic industry, they charged: Instead, its "partnership" scheme systematically pits worker against worker, destroying solidarity and weakening the union. Saturn rank-and-file activist Tom Hopp calls the resulting system "worse than the company unions in the Thirties." Management makes a point of not listening, the local union doesn't put up much of a fight, and workers suffer.

the floor, doors and steering column. Even standing still the Seville has engineering problems: It can't be shifted into low gear when you're using the cup holder. That's right: a $55,000 piece of shit.

But that doesn't really matter. Cadillac is a company built on dreams, and it is dying because it has so grossly misinterpreted the dreams of the post-Sixties middle men and women. Over the course of the century, Cadillac invested millions in building a fantasy of American aristocracy, but up-and-comers today like to see themselves more in the vein of Beats and bikers than titans and CEOs. The new swells don't care about the "Penalty of Leadership"—they imagine themselves breaking from the pack altogether; they dream that they're "free agents" roaming the corporate landscape, rebels who, but for a small twist of fate, would be writing poetry or racing their hog instead of putting together reports on investment prospects in the skin-care industry. Pity poor Cadillac with their double-ton whales and their baggage of respectability and privilege—today's strivers wouldn't be caught dead in one. They've moved over to the sportier, sexier (and let's be honest, better made) BMW and Lexus. For probably the first time in history, the bourgeoisie does not want to appear bourgeois—they want to party.

Perhaps if Cadillac had stuck it out with the tailfins back in '59; if they had weathered the contempt of their traditional customers and sloughed the corporate vice-presidential buyer off on Buick, they wouldn't be in such terrible shape today. But that's just not Cadillac's nature, and as things stand they're faced with a long, long game of catch-up. Unfortunately, though, the company's repeated bids for the with-it dollar have generated nothing but a pitiful parade of failure:

❦ 1975. Cadillac introduces the downsized Seville (built up from a Nova) in response to the oil crisis and the first wave of imports. It bombs, its value depreciating 21 percent its first year (compared to Nova's 4 percent).

❦ 1980. Cadillac attempts to resuscitate the Seville with the "Elegante" line. While its advertising speaks of it as "quite possibly the most distinctive car in the world today," GM designers—evidently bereft of any other ideas—appear simply to have sawed off the trunk at a forty-five degree angle. Two-tone paint jobs introduced later in schemes like "Desert Dusk Firemist over Brownstone" don't help any, and the new butt-less Sevilles continue to lose nearly a quarter of their value.

❦ 1982. Enter the Cimarron, four cylinders and four feet shorter than the previous models. Unfortunately, Cadillac can't convince buyers to pay luxury car prices for a gussied-up Chevy Cavalier, the ass-end workhorse of car rental fleets. Openly discussed in the industry as a "disaster," the Cimarron is discontinued by the end of the decade.

❦ 1997. The Caddy That Zigs: the Catera. An Americanized Opel manufactured in Europe, the Catera is designed to win over the newest generation of young bucks rollerblading over the carcass of bourgeois sobriety. But as with their previous forays into the class consciousness of the new breed of rebel accountants, Cadillac's aim has been less than spot-on. They walked into a shitstorm when they unveiled the Catera during the 1997 Super Bowl with an ad featuring Cindy Crawford as a leather-clad dominatrix. Cadillac's own female executives publicly castigated the campaign. So Cadillac immediately fishtailed from a pitiable idea of sexiness to an equally pathetic notion of cuteness: a

But the reality that's carried the day is the one invented for Saturn by its ad agency, the ultra-creative firm of Hal Riney and Partners. One commercial introduced some new Saturn models by relating how the plant closed down for a couple days to "make a few changes." Everyone got new safety glasses, the cafeteria started serving chili cheese dogs, and a new basket went onto the basketball rim. The team members sauntered back in—only to find that the plant has been retooled to produce new models!

The new models themselves arrive in the commercial almost as an afterthought, reminding consumers of how other auto manufacturers play up their new designs. Here things are different: It's **the plant itself**—not the product—that's the intended focus of the ad. Americans bought the labor-relations-as-corporate-philosophy thing, they bought the new myth of the happy team member, and they bought the cars. In 1992, Saturn sold more cars per franchise than any other make in the United States.

The Spring Hill plant does in fact utilize a relatively new management theory, the "team concept." According to the official line, Saturn "team members" have input on all decisions: which vehicles to produce, how to set up work stations, what times are appropriate for breaks. "Saturn's a different kind of company," according to the corporate Web site. "It's built on partnerships and teamwork and a belief that a good idea can come from any one of us. It's a pretty revolutionary approach," one that keeps the cars advanced and the workers "involved and inspired."

Indeed, workers at Saturn labor under a "living agreement" very different from the standard contract that governs relations between GM and the United Auto Workers at other plants. The Saturn contract was ratified by the union in 1985 (several years before any of the employees who would work under it were hired), at a time when American companies were finding that threats of plant closings brought easy concessions from unions. At the same time, the UAW leadership was coming to believe that foreign competition justified signing on with management's new "competitiveness" schemes. Longtime labor activist and former UAW regional director Jerry Tucker recalls how one high-ranking union leader shot down criticism of the team concept by insisting, "It's our job to make these corporations lean and mean!" Such talk was common in those days. In a 1984 address to a gathering of auto execs, union official Donald Ephlin claimed that the UAW was enthusiastic for the Saturn project "because we think it will finally symbolize that we are in the fight to stay and we are serious about being competitive."

Under the Saturn contract—commonly known as the "little gray book"—the union was made a full partner in all decisions from new equipment to break times, democratically elected shop

bicycle-riding cartoon spokesduck (an "irreverent" takeoff on the regal birds of the Cadillac crest, says David Nitolli, Catera's brand manager). No opera houses or subservient minions, furs or suits, sell these Cadillacs: Instead, the car is described as a "whole new omelet" and introduced with cutesy homilies about Catera-owning iconoclasts, like the big sister who "always did things a little differently." But The Caddy That Zigs is still a Caddy, and next to a Lexus or BMW it looks like the sorry son of blubber it is.

Ironically, the Catera is reported to be a pretty good car, garnering positive reviews from consumer groups. But Cadillac, of all companies, should know that the physical product is secondary to the phantasmagoric identity it projects. And the tale the Catera tells is one of neither master aristocrat nor irreverent entrepreneur. It's the autobiography of a portly middle-aged man with hair plugs, sweating on the dance floor and cheating on his wife. The Catera is politely referred to in the press as a "disappointment in the show room" (read: not selling), and the average age of its buyers is fifty-eight.

III.

IN 1998 John Smith, Cadillac's general manager, announced that Cadillac would soon be introducing a "lifestyle vehicle." In other words, a sport utility vehicle, nay, the Cadillac of sport utility vehicles, the largest SUV on the road. Built up from the GMC Yukon, Caddy's road tank weighs in at about three tons, outsizing even their prime steroidic competitor, the Lincoln Navigator. After considering names like "Commander," "Conquistador," and, I kid you not, "Revolution," Cadillac settled on the rather understated "Escalade" (the word means to rise or climb, as in "we desperately need escalating sales"). They should have stuck with "Revolution."

The SUV is another chance for Caddy to speak to the dreams—and nightmares—of the wannabe American aristocracy. This new Caddy, like all other SUVs, will no doubt be sold with images of mountains being climbed, rivers forded, deserts crossed, and jungles conquered—the fantasies of freedom that fill the daydreams of the desk jockey. Maybe it will appeal to the rebellious BMW-buying hearts of those who would be the new ruling class.

But as with most SUVs, the only jungle this Caddy will ever face will be the urban jungle, the one whose natives so haunt the nightmares of the new aspirants. The income gap is widening and the safety net has collapsed. Those former Ford-buying masses are slipping back to what in the nineteenth century were quaintly called the "dangerous classes." Having recently relocated their headquarters to the Renaissance Center, located in 80 percent black and overwhelmingly poor downtown Detroit, General Motors executives know the terror. And the natives are getting restless: Recalling their militant past, the United Auto Workers struck GM plants over half a dozen times last year. Appropriately enough, the largest strike was triggered by management's decision to move the metal-stamping dies for their "lifestyle vehicles" out of their Flint, Michigan plant to cheaper lands. Workers effectively shut down GM production across the United States, Canada, and Mexico. "Envy, fear, greed, ambition and the desire to surpass" howl at the gates of the managerial class.

With the Escalade, Cadillac is returning to its roots. Once again they're promising the arriviste a way out of the very class system through which they've risen. But there's a difference this time: The separation that Cadillac is selling these days is made of heavy-gauge steel. Insulate, insulate, insulate was the mantra of Tom Wolfe's "masters of the universe" back in the Eighties: For the most part, the new master class can stay safe inside the walls of their gated communities, order out for food, and telecommute to work, living in exile from the brutal world they created and which created them. But sooner or later—perhaps when nothing good is playing on pay-per-view—they'll have to venture out. And then there's that other day lurking on the edge of every corporatron's consciousness, the day when the bubble pops and the "dangerous classes" begin to regard them as a symbol of what they don't have. What better vehicle for such special occasions than a rolling ruling-class survivalist compound, a super-lux SUV. As long as there's inequality, Cadillac's future is assured. Introducing the new Escalade: The Caddy for the Class War. 🖼

stewards were replaced with jointly appointed worker representatives, standard GM hourly pay was thrown out in favor of a lower base pay augmented with performance bonuses, and shop-floor rules were all but replaced with loose agreements to work together on all problems. Many of the gains won by the union over the past fifty years—clearly stated shop-floor rules that hemmed in management's power to abuse, exploit, and intimidate employees—were replaced with promises to work and play together nicely.

The recent strike vote came about after Saturn management repeatedly reneged on these pledges. In July 1998, GM announced that it would build future Saturn models outside of Spring Hill, using parts from other GM plants. According to Spring Hill UAW shop-committee chairman Mike Bennett—hardly an outspoken critic of management—the new models were planned without any input from the union. "What's a Saturn," the **Wall Street Journal** quoted him saying, "if it's not built on a Saturn platform by Saturn workers?" The vote, though a sign of nearly unanimous worker discontent, led nowhere: After the GM strike in Flint, Michigan was settled last summer, the union's international leadership was reluctant to authorize any more work stoppages.

If shop-floor climate is any indication, another strike vote at Saturn could come soon. Observers of life on the line at Saturn (and other plants organized according to the team concept) have repeatedly described a climate of fear. As one worker told a **New York Times** reporter who toured the plant in the summer of 1998, "I've got a dozen team members who are going to get on my case if I don't do my job properly." By replacing standard hourly pay with team-wide performance bonuses, the Saturn system puts peer pressure on team

Continued on page 48

Not the town

as in a colonial outpost
local do-good cablers
on pass-the-microphone-tv
make Rimbaud's
"oxidize the gargoyles"
sound like the butler
in the "Red Dwarf"—
not the town,
the walls, are painted red
for years & years
the households suffer
bloated ill-temperament,
the way personal crises
can continue in an
underlying manner—
the reminder is
"don't ignore the abject."
that reminds me—
these parliamentary candidates
are those Baudrillard
would call
   "a conjuration
   of imbeciles"—
chaotic music backgrounds
their flaggy luncheons,
their floral tributes
deny any opposition,
their militaristic hobbies—
fokkerschmidt submachine
diesel boot the bottom line.
scanning the windows
of Cash Converters
for stolen cell phones,
the ground trembles
as traffic exits the shopping
complex parking station,
in fuck-the-reader-Timezone
the premature ejaculators,
their fingers on the game,
hoot for joy every time
they destroy another animation.

—Pam Brown

Dipping Extremely Low in the Lap of Corporate Luxury

A Sell-Out's Tale

BRYANT URSTADT

The Invitation

ONE day last February I got a message from a woman named Jennifer. As messages go, it was a good one. She worked for Volvo Cars of North America, and she wanted to fly me to Phoenix for a three-day stay in a first-class hotel, all expenses paid.

She had a nice voice. Her message was short. She said: "You are preregistered for the Volvo C70 introduction in Phoenix. Can you call me back to work out the flight details?"

It would have been a cryptic message, but I had already been on one Volvo press trip, and I knew immediately that I had just been offered a cushy vacation. All Volvo wanted, in return, was for me to mention their car in a national publication. Or, to put it bluntly, all they wanted was my journalistic integrity.

She left an 800-number so that I could call her to schedule my free vacation without putting a dime on my phone bill. Volvo, as always, had thought of everything. As well they should have done. Like all the major automakers, when Volvo introduces a new car, or even a model change, they fly hundreds of journalists to a carefully scouted exotic

location, put them up in royal style, and wait for the glowing reviews. I just had to tell her I would go.

I called Jennifer back.

"Hi. This is Bryant Urstadt. I'm calling about the Volvo trip."

"Yes. Will you be leaving from LaGuardia or Kennedy? Do you have any airline you prefer?"

I preferred any airline anywhere—I had been stuck staring out my New York tenement window for months—but I held my tongue. She was asking because most journalists use these trips to rack up frequent-flier miles.

"Actually, I just wanted to know a little more about the trip."

"Volvo is introducing journalists to their new C70 line of convertibles. The trip is three days in Phoenix, test-driving the convertibles. If you fly out of Kennedy you can go direct."

"A convertible? That sounds nice. Can I call you back? I'm not sure I've been assigned to write about the C70."

"That's no problem, I'll keep your space open."

I spent a good part of the next day trying to figure out whether to take Volvo up on their offer. Of course I wanted to kick around

Continued from page 45
members who either miss work or can't make quota. Furthermore, since workers help decide on the distribution of tasks, when more work is added each team fights to get it assigned to others. As Tom Hopp puts it, team-concept plants turn each small bunch of workers into "their own little group of piranhas." Management in such plants doesn't need to do much to police the line—workers keep themselves on target.

The recent vote for new leadership resulted from years of rank-and-file organizing by Hopp and others. They argue that the Saturn "partnership," by eliminating the old system of shop-floor rules, contributes to a high number of on-the-job injuries. They accuse local union leaders of disregarding union members' rights, pointing to an incident in which 51 employees of the paint shop had their jobs eliminated without warning. Most importantly, they demand the standard union benefits that the unique Saturn contract has eliminated: higher pay, elected representatives, and clear shop-floor rules.

The newly elected head of Local 1853, Robert Williams, was the only local union official to side with activists during last year's campaign to adopt the standard UAW-GM contract and jettison the "little gray book." His slate, which Hopp helped organize, didn't promise a new contract altogether. But according to **The New York Times**, the new leadership would like to adopt many work rules from other GM plants.

It's been a long, hard battle. A story in **Labor Notes** recalls the massive obstacles faced by those working on last year's "reversion" campaign: They were denied access to the union hall, and the president of Spring Hill Local 1853 declared on the plant's in-house TV station that reversion would cause the plant to close.

Still, the insurgents persevered, and they've managed to put new leaders into

Phoenix for three days in a convertible. But I had always considered myself a serious person, serious enough to quit my job and write at home, giving up a salary, health care, companionship, and a killer view of downtown Manhattan to fashion my art in solitude, or something like that. Serious writers aren't supposed to suck the corporate teat. They are not supposed to do anything but try and pinch it with a clothespin, or chafe it somehow. *The New York Times*, *Rolling Stone* and every other "serious" publication forbids their writers to take so much as a free lunch from a corporation.

It's not hard to figure out why publications like these forbid their writers to go on press trips: How seriously would you take my opinion on the Volvo XC All-Wheel-Drive wagon if you knew that last summer I had been flown out to Alaska, served salmon on top of a glacier reached by cable car, given a fishing rod, shooting lessons and an all-weather reversible jacket with detachable liner, among other things? If you were feeling principled, you might think it didn't matter what I said about that car, or about anything else.

I resolved the matter with a nice bit of doublethink. I would go to Phoenix and write an article, but not about the wonders of the C70 convertible (although I might have to touch on that), but about how Volvo gets people to write about the wonders of the C70. I would be a spy, you see, and not just another hack fighting for his share of the corporate sow's tasty milk.

Still, I hadn't entirely convinced myself. I may have explained to colleagues that I was headed to Phoenix to expose the phenomenon of the press trip, but I was really dreaming of the sun lighting the prickly arms of the *saguaros* as it dipped behind the sandy mountains of the desert, and wondering if, in the heat of Arizona, the women would be wearing tank tops and cut-off jeans.

Volvo, in the person of their travel agent, Jennifer, seemed delighted to hear from me when I called the next day.

"Mr. Urstadt! I'm glad you called."

In her gracious manner, she beckoned me deeper into the warm and fluffy corporate bosom.

"Would you be going March 24 to 26, or March 31 through April 2?"

"What's the difference?"

"The first wave is lifestyle reporters. The second wave will all be from the automotive papers."

The Alaska trip had been filled with automotive reporters, and I had had my fill of stories about heroically maxing-out some hot car on the test track in Stuttgart, so I chose to join the somewhat anemic-sounding "lifestyle" group.

"Lifestyle" includes all of those publications one reads to better fit into some group, to "live" better in some way. *GQ* would qualify, since it teaches you how to be a better man; *Family Life* would, too, because it teaches you how to be a better parent, and so on through *Modern Bride, Cosmopolitan, Glamour*, et cetera. It's a genre that produces journalists no less annoying than the automotive geek variety—and even more reliable for Volvo's purposes. Fifteen lifestyle journalists can be dispatched to write about the same subject and generate—working alone in their own offices, spread across the continent, with only a few press releases and their own experience as a guide—fifteen nearly identical articles.

There were to be ten waves of reporters, in groups of about thirty, aimed at a huge span of markets, including South Americans, Japanese, Europeans and, in its own wave, Brazilians. The American lifestyle writers would be about the fifth wave, after the technogeeks, before the Japanese.

"Do you have any special requests for your hotel room?"

In my life, I have only ever made one request of a hotel room, and that is that it be as cheap as possible. That wasn't what she was asking.

"I'd like it to be pretty big, I guess."

She laughed. "I'm sure you'll find it comfortable. Any special pillows or anything?"

"Special pillows?"

"Yes?"

"No. I think regular pillows would be fine. Soft, though."

Jennifer called up a few mornings later. She left a message saying I should call her immediately. Naturally, I did. She needed to know my jacket size. Volvo, she explained, wanted to give me a windbreaker with their logo on the breast. I had been needing a windbreaker.

office. Now comes the real challenge: Dealing with GM, whose plans to build future models outside of Spring Hill using parts from other plants is what triggered the strike-authorization vote last July. Today GM is seeking concessions—likely more pay-for-performance initiatives—in exchange for keeping the Saturn factory where it is. Although Local 1853 members have shown that they're serious about getting their power and dignity back, the company might downgrade production at their plant if they put up too much of a fight. Years of organizing might come to naught.

Not coincidentally, the Saturn organizational model continues to spread to other plants. Two years ago, GM moved Skip LeFauve from VP in charge of Saturn to a position overseeing efforts to create a single GM "corporate culture" and develop standard nationwide management practices. GM also runs a consulting firm to help other corporations learn the team concept.

GM clearly sees Saturn as its model for the future, simultaneously allowing it to control movements for workplace democracy and to speak to a new breed of consumer. Before the counterculture and the oil crises messed everything up, GM had a fairly simple marketing scheme: Its different divisions were tailor-made for groups differentiated by age, wealth, and status. Youngsters went for the Chevy, or the sportier Pontiac. With age and power came classier autos: the Buick, then the Oldsmobile, then finally the Cadillac.

As established power loses its cool, several GM lines are floundering, their identities confused or even repulsive to a more sensitive generation of consumers. Successful brands these days match up with personal "tastes" connected less to consumers' age or status than their personal identity. Saturn is GM's attempt to integrate the new logic of marketing. Its customers aren't defined by a single age or income bracket, but by a sensibility.

They know that consumerism is bad and that it hurts the environment, but they still need to drive to work every day. They like the fact that Saturn has taken the time to give single workers that most precious of liberal possessions, an individual voice. They distrust the powerful, but aren't sure why workplace organization is a good thing.

They're the same well-educated, culturally radical, conflict-despising "progressives" who patronize any number of brands that talk a socially responsible game. A Saturn is a natural for this kind of consumer: It marks the buyer as both economically sensible and culturally astute. To drive one is to help break down the old hierarchies of wealth, gender, and power. Saturn owners are unabashed egalitarians. Saturn's appeal is exactly in that it's not your father's Oldsmobile.

And how they love that company! In the summer of 1994, GM invited Saturn buyers down to Spring Hill for a two-day "Homecoming," which also served as a photo-op for the ad folks. Apparently without being paid, some 44,000 gave up their traditional trips to the lake and headed back to the ol' farm. They did some line-dancing, ate some soul food, and met some other Saturn owners who, they found out, they really have an awful lot in common with. During the factory tours, they got to learn all sorts of interesting things about how their cars were made. They even got to meet some of the folks who'd put their cars together, and hear what they thought about the team concept.

They're really, really glad they went. They sure needed to get away from it all for a bit.

A month or two later, at around 11:30 in the morning, the FedEx man arrived, and handed me a package. Inside was an envelope, from "Volvo Travel Headquarters," stamped, "Important Travel Information Enclosed."

I paused to reflect on my temporary grandeur: Important travel information, delivered by courier, to my door. It was just how I wanted to live.

The envelope contained a custom Volvo luggage tag, my airline tickets, and a letter from Volvo Travel Headquarters, welcoming me to "sunny Phoenix, Arizona" and explaining that the luggage tag would "expedite handling." Also included was a brochure from the Royal Palms Hotel and Casitas, a hotel which appears to represent the highest achievement in the art of prefab elegance. Finally, there was "The 1998 Volvo C70 Convertible Lifestyle Media Program Event Agenda." This document—its wonderful title hinting at the deadly serious precision which Volvo applied to making sure journalists had "fun"—offered not one, but two agendas.

There was Program A, which included a guided tour of Frank Lloyd Wright's Taliesin West, a visit to a vintage airplane restorer, and lunch with survival expert J.D. Holman, and Program B, which included a drive to the red cliffs of Sedona, known by locals as the "cosmic center of the world," followed by a visit to an artist at the Mountain Trails Gallery who specialized in Native American themes. In addition to Native American "inspired" art, Program B also threatened to expose me to Lily Dorene Falk, whose "exquisitely crafted creations are worn by celebrities and other high-profile, fashion-conscious clients," so I chose program A. Both programs seemed a little strange until one considered them in the larger context of Volvo's current image campaign, which aims to reach a "sensitive," educated, semi-affluent consumer. Or as one of their many press releases put it, the "individualist."

When my girlfriend got home from work, she examined the brochure from the Royal Palms. It was

about twenty degrees fahrenheit in New York that day.

"I can't believe you're going there," she said, with real envy.

The Journey

ARRIVING in Phoenix's grandly named Sky Harbor International Airport, I was greeted by a driver holding up a sign with my name on it. His name was Ron and he was the first man to ever hold up a sign for me. He had scribbled my name in highlighter, and I could barely read it, but that did nothing to diminish the flattery of the gesture. Ron wore a white short-sleeved shirt, a black tie and black pants. He shook my hand and we were off, trundling down the endless airport corridors. As I followed him, he began talking about Phoenix the way a tour guide might, giving me details about its founding, and the average yearly temperature and rainfall. He was one of the only Volvo-related people I would meet who didn't treat me as though I was one of the most important people on earth.

After driving me through miles of Jiffy Lubes, RiteAids and Wal-Marts, Ron delivered me unto the Royal Palms Hotel. Volvo's people had spent months choosing the right hotel, and whatever image it exuded reflected careful decisions on the part of the trip-planners. The Royal Palms keeps out the public with a pink adobe wall circling the perimeter of one block in Phoenix. To enter, we passed through an iron gate which looked like it might have been stolen from the set of *Citizen Kane*. The crunchy gravel driveway circled

around a verdant flowerbed. Sitting out by the front doors were two teal Volvo C70 convertibles and a sky-blue Volvo convertible dating from 1956.

A blond woman at the register welcomed me with great warmth, gave my key to the bellhop, and explained that Volvo had taken care of the tipping.

"That's what I like to hear," I said, possibly too enthusiastically.

The bellhop was ruddy, chipper, and so happy that I suspected that Volvo must have *really* taken care of the tipping. He picked up my light bag, asked me how my flight was and told me how I could get whatever I wanted at a number of locations.

My room was just off the pool. The bellhop laid my bag down on a special bag holder at the foot of my bed. He pointed out a pile of fruit in a basket. "That's fresh," he said, "I made sure this morning. I'll bet it'll taste pretty good after hours of traveling."

With a few obsequious nods, telling me to call him if I needed anything, he actually backed out of the room, leaving me alone to admire it.

The room was marvelously appointed in the Southwestern mode, with a Navajo-style rug on the floor, an ornate hutch holding the television and minibar, and a heavy wood desk with swirling Spanish-style legs. The bathroom, too, was elegantly laid out, with its own desk. The toilet paper was folded into an arrow at the first square. And on one side of the sink was a stack of freshly laundered, expertly folded towels.

The desk in the main room was heaped with gifts from Volvo. Beside the bowl of fresh fruit, there was a custom boutique bag, in Volvo blue, emblazoned with a photograph of the C70 in the desert at sunset, under the motto, "Volvo C70 Convertible—Tan Safely." Inside the bag was a tube of sunblock, a tastefully pre-weathered beige baseball cap, and a new pair of Ray-Ban Wayfarers (approximate retail price $75). Also on the desk was my jacket, a brand-new beige windbreaker with "Volvo" stitched into the breast, and a fancy folder filled with four-color glossy press material about Volvo and the C70, including an expensive-looking magazine called "Open Mind, The Volvo C70 Convertible Magazine," also available on an enclosed CD-ROM.

The hotel's Palmera Lounge, where the introductory remarks were scheduled for that evening, was less lounge than an open breezeway, and Volvo had taken advantage of its spacious opening by wheeling in a special version of the C70 convertible and surrounding it with conference chairs. The body panels from this particular C70 had been removed to reveal impressive-looking structural features— the extra safety measures Volvo is known for—which were highlighted with bright yellow paint. Here I got my first introduction to the Volvo corporate employees. They were not hard to spot. Besides looking almost comically Swedish—straw-haired, azure-eyed, and much-reddened by the Southwestern sun—they were also all wearing black pants topped with a saffron short-sleeve buttondown, both embossed with the Volvo C70

logo. There were a few American employees of Volvo mixed in, also in Volvo uniforms. The Americans, I must say, looked a little shaggy compared to the Swedish.

Among the lifestyle editors and journalists there was an air of giddy hilarity. We all must have felt like we had been getting away with something, standing there on the pink adobe stairs that led to the Palmera Lounge in balmy Phoenix. We were all wearing the name tags the Volvo publicity people had left in our hotel rooms. Several of us were from New York, and we made jokes about the grim weather we had left behind. There was Penny, the managing editor of an enormous bride's magazine; Heidi and Andrea, both automobile reporters for a New York tabloid; and other authors or editors from a wide variety of lifestyle periodicals like *Bikini, Washington CEO, GQ, Good Housekeeping* and *Flair*, a Canadian fashion magazine.[†]

Ree Hartwell, Volvo's media relations manager, was also there and she looked happy to see me, though it was hard to gauge her true feelings, since it was her job to look happy to see me. Ree looked happy to see me because I was officially representing *Family Life*, a publication aimed at parents of kids from three to twelve. The magazine tries to reach readers with higher household incomes—readers that interest Volvo very much. With a circulation of five hundred thousand, a nice spread on the Volvo convertible would more than pay for my trip.

---

† All together there were about thirty of us. I've done my best to conceal the identities of the writers by changing their names, trying to balance the importance of naming the publications with a desire to protect the other writers. Like me, they probably went into journalism for decent reasons, and got battered along the way by the meagerness of their incomes.

We all settled into conference chairs ranged around the special C70. On each chair lay a sand-colored Volvo pad and a black-and-chrome mechanical pencil/pen with Volvo stamped on the lead-dispensing button.

With these gifts we were to record the words of José Diaz de la Vega, the chief designer of the C70's interiors and color trim. Diaz de la Vega's speech was high theater, a campy mélange of catchphrases and carefully designed slogans. Diaz de la Vega spoke in a way that reminded me of Ricardo Montalban. He frequently spread his hands for emphasis, and to make the transition between points, brought his hands together in a kind of prayer gesture. He frequently laid these same hands on the special C70 in a loving way. (I kept hoping that he might brush its supple, fragrant upholstery with the back of his hand, and purr about its "rich Corinthian leather.")

As for Diaz de la Vega's disquisition—some drivel about the "six senses" Volvo engineers had in mind when designing the C70—I was, after a few minutes, on the verge of tuning out completely. As he mimed his slogans with expertly faked passion, I drifted off into my own thoughts behind that polite, blank face one gives when one is being delivered information one doesn't want. In the chairs around me, however, I noticed my colleagues busily scribbling, some into their new Volvo pads, most into reporter-style notebooks. It occurred to me that Diaz de la Vega's palaver might well show up in C70 reviews (it did), and so I started taking notes as well. The Volvo pads, it turned out, were not just a gift, they were a push in what Volvo considered the right direction. They couldn't literally write our reviews for us, but they were willing to dictate.

Diaz de la Vega concluded his talk with a few polished remarks, which had been polished, no doubt, in costly brainstorming sessions with the "creatives." Among these gems were, "Many convertibles have the looks, but few have the brains," "This isn't the Volvo you need, it's the Volvo you want," and his final remark, which we heard and saw over and over again during our stay, "Tan safely."

After the introductory remarks, we were led out to a phalanx of buses, which took us to the Wrigley Mansion on the outskirts of Phoenix. I boarded and sat down next to Heidi, one of the writers for the New York tabloid. She was middle-aged,

and wore a T-shirt with a big black cat on it. I asked her if she went on these trips a lot. She said she did, and that with various manufacturers she had been flown all over the States, to Europe on the Concorde, and once to Japan. The car manufacturers, she related, were currently in a mini-war of extravagance, competing to be the most lavish and the most inviting, and lately the trips, along with the economy, had been getting better and better. It was a pretty good deal, we agreed. She asked me if I would be writing about Volvo. I said I would.

"What's your angle?"

"I think I'm going to be writing about press trips in general."

"An exposé?" She asked, sounding worried.

"Sort of, I guess."

"Don't ruin it for the rest of us," she said, without a trace of humor.

At the Wrigley Mansion we gathered for a four-course meal in the grand dining room overlooking the ten miles of plain leading to Phoenix. There were a number of writers at my table, and a few Volvo reps. The mood, again, was of the highest joy, as though we were all lottery winners, assembled to be congratulated for our good luck and to be awarded the cash prize.

Over white wine and dessert, a goblet full of fresh berries, and to the soft tinkle of a pianist playing "You Are So Beautiful," the conversation turned to the press trips themselves. Heidi was at my table, and at some point mentioned that she had writer friends, who, when the press people called up to invite them on a trip, asked first, "What are the gifts?" If her friends didn't like the gifts, they wouldn't go. This launched a whole round of press trip stories. The writers had been flown all over the world. Mexico had flown them to Mexico, so that they would write good things about Mexico, and so on, through a whole raft of countries, cars, and more general products. They compared gifts and joked about how many frequent-flier miles they had accumulated. I tried to join in—I had a plush bathrobe from Nickelodeon, and some khaki pants from when the Gap was "introducing" khakis and sent a pair to just about every editor in Manhattan—but I had more to add about my friends than myself. I knew people who had been sent to "check out" the South of France, Scotland, exclusive islands in Florida and the Caribbean. (Anyone sick enough to read the hundreds of magazines that come out each month will pick up on certain mini-trends in travel articles, usually sparked by the enthusiasm of writers who have just flown there on the country's tab.) Writers I had met on the trip to Alaska had been flown to Sweden to test Saabs, given BMWs to drive in Bavaria, and so on.

My best story, though, was about an editor I had worked for in New York. She wrote travel stories, and went to several ranches and ski areas—all expenses paid—with her family several times a year. She was scrupulous about kissing their asses. As her assistant, I was constantly sending out clips of her obsequious articles to the ranches she had been to, as thanks and insurance that she would be invited back. I also sent her clips to places she hadn't yet visited, in hopes of an invitation. Her office was literally filled with gifts from companies. They were piled up against every wall, in garish stacks on her desk, under her desk, blocking her door—books, tapes, CDs, software, complicated plastic toys, sports equipment, clothes, and on and on. Many of them were duplicates, for she had been in touch with so many companies for so long that she was frequently on their mailing lists twice, but I never once saw her part with one single gift, no matter how many she had or how irrelevant it was to her life. In contrast to her Scrooge-like personal habits was the witty, fun-loving voice of her articles, which no doubt sent thousands of her several hundred thousand readers flocking to the ranches, ski areas, and product lines of her corporate friends. After a while, I realized that maybe it was a story I shouldn't have been telling, and with so much disdain, to the particular table I was at, so I decided to be quiet for a bit.

Penny from the wedding magazine was at my table, too. She had also been on Volvo's Alaska trip. A little while after my rant, I asked her how a car review would fit in a magazine aimed at newlyweds. Did they recommend cars for newlyweds?

"I made it into a kind of travel thing," she said. "You know, Alaska for the honeymoon."

"Did you mention Volvo?"

She had. And she would probably be working a similar angle for this trip.

When I got back to my room, my sheets had been folded back, a plush bathrobe had been laid out on my bed, and on my pillow was a foil-wrapped mint, with Volvo stamped into the chocolate. I didn't eat it.

The next morning, the journalists of the North American lifestyle wave of the C70 rollout ate breakfast at T. Cook's restaurant, flipping through the complimentary *USA Today*s. As for T. Cook's, I will let the hotel's own material describe it. "A stunning view of Camelback Mountain and a grand wood burning fireplace will take your breath away. The perfect setting for our rustic Mediterranean fare." And at night, the brochure continues, the pianist "plays your favorite 'oldies' and the bartender remembers your 'usual' in an atmosphere that evokes warm memories of recent years past."

I sat with a couple of the younger writers, including Ben, who worked for *Rolling Stone Online*, which

strictly bars their employees from hopping press trips. Ben had taken the trip for another magazine. Writing for a publication that forbids trips, and going under the name of another, seemed quite common.

He was a friendly guy, a hip, recently arrived New Yorker. He wore a black T-shirt, jeans, and fat black leather shoes with lug soles. He had his hair cut short in a spiky do. The trip was cool, he said, but he was just using it to get to L.A., so he could visit his girlfriend. He had somehow convinced Volvo to fly him through L.A., with Phoenix as a stopover. Not that Volvo had needed much convincing. As far as I could tell, they would bend in just about any direction if the possibility of coverage was at stake.

Afterward, we assembled at the Palmera Meeting Room, just off the Palmera Lounge. There we were given spiral-bound "Road Books" with "Volvo Phoenix 1998" on the cover. Inside were detailed directions to Taliesin West, the Carefree Air Park Estate, Bartlett Lake and back to the Royal Palms, accompanied by a fold-out road map and important telephone numbers.

Out front were fifteen brand new convertibles, in shimmering metallic gold, each with about ten miles on the odometer and the keys in the ignition. The writers stood around while Volvo's audio test engineer, Andreas Gustafson, showed us journalists how to work both the three-CD magazines and the larger, six-CD changer in the trunk. Andreas and his team had gone so far as to compile special CD mixes of driving music, with uptempo tunes like Abba's "Dancing Queen" and the single from Madonna's "Ray of Light."

Of course, it was important to choose someone cool to drive with, so I matched up with Ben, because at breakfast he had been brandishing a case of CDs.

Thus briefed, Ben and I pulled out of the Royal Palms, and headed south to Taliesin West, one-time headquarters of Frank Lloyd Wright. I drove. I suppose I had some seniority since I had been on the press trip to Alaska and he had not. This was his first trip. Ben sat in the passenger seat with Volvo's careful directions open on his lap.

We pulled out into the Phoenix traffic.

"Hey," I said. "Could you pass me my Wayfarers?"

"You're going to wear those things?" he said.

"I know, they're stupid, but it's too sunny out. My eyes are sensitive."

He handed me the Wayfarers, and stubbornly squinted for about two blocks, and then put his pair on too. Suddenly we were two young guys in a brand-new $45,000 metallic-gold convertible, both wearing Wayfarers.

People stared at us at the stoplights and on the freeways. One guy yelled out the window of his BMW to tell us that we had some cool wheels. We both gave him a big, friendly thumbs-up. As cars pulled alongside and their drivers examined us, I felt like I was riding a thin line between having everyone want to know me and getting the shit beaten out of me by four teenagers in a chopped muscle car.

But it was impossible to be too cynical about the car. We were both delighted to be, for once, the ones on the other side, the ones in the fast car, the car that got the looks.

The C70 drove beautifully, although it was, in its essentials, identical to most every other car ever made, in that it was able to stop and start and turn, on demand. At one stoplight, I gunned it.

"Good pickup on this baby," I said.

"Yeah, and the stereo kicks butt," said Ben.

Once I pressed the brakes really hard and screeched to a stop.

"Stops nice," I said.

"Yeah, seems good," said Ben.

Neither of us had any idea what we were talking about, in terms of automobiles, and we immediately admitted to one another that we had no intention of writing about the car, and that we were both simply taking advantage of a free trip.

After a private tour of Taliesin, we were served a box lunch with bubbly water, sitting in a private courtyard under umbrellas. Afterward Ben drove and I gave him the directions in our road book, which took us to the Carefree Airpark, a paved strip of desert on the outskirts of town. When we arrived, a World War II P-51 Mustang roared off the runaway and tipped its wings at us. We gave him a honk.

Once the plane had taken off, we were left alone in a performance car on a runway.

"What do you think?" asked Ben. "Should I see what this can do?"

"Yeah." I made sure my seat belt was tight, and he hit the gas. We launched down the runway, and hit a top speed of 120 before Ben let up.

"Jesus, what a rush," he said.

I thought for a moment of what I would be doing if, as journalists, we had done the "right" thing, and stayed in New York. I saw myself at my little desk, hunched over my computer, occasionally glancing up at the fire escapes out my window.

After our speed trials, the other Volvo-testers started to show up in their C70s and we gathered by an airplane hangar, where a salty old guy showed us his 1943 Steadman biplane and let us sit in the cockpit.

Then we drove up into the mountains, dutifully following Volvo's entertainment schedule, and met another character hired by Volvo, a fellow by the name of J.D. Holman. He was dressed in period costume dating from about 1880—down to antique pocket watch, handlebar moustache, and ivory-handled pistol—and he gave us a well-rehearsed lecture on the dangers of

the desert. Maricopa County Deputy Sheriff Stoner showed up, although we never really knew why. Volvo must have hired him for some reason. Deputy Sheriff Stoner was very nice about helping J.D.'s wife serve us bottled water and home-made cookies.

At every event, we were joined by several of Volvo's people, who answered our simple questions—"How many cylinders does it have?"—with grace and enthusiasm. They, too, were tooling around in brand-new C70s, and seemed to be having as much fun as we were. Again, they all wore a uniform; they seemed to have had a different one made for each segment of the event. This time their outfit included black C70-embossed hiking shorts and a T-shirt with a picture of a pair of Wayfarers hanging off the end of the words "Cruise Brothers."

I asked Andreas, the audio guy, about the T-shirt.

"It's just for fun. Our guys, they like uniforms. They get an idea, they just do it."

In the afternoon, having finally escaped the pre-planned activities of Program A, Ben and I took off into the mountains surrounding Phoenix. We happened on a state park, and climbed to the top of a hill. There was an abandoned Native American settlement there, six or seven hundred years old. Far below we could see our C70, looking absurdly luxurious alone in the small parking lot. Mountains and hills stretched out in every direction, reaching up to drifting clouds. The warm feelings for Volvo were overwhelming. Volvo had given us all of this.

That night was the big dinner, at the Royal Palms, in the Estrella Salon by the reflecting pool. Most overnight press trips have their big dinner, where the journalists mix with the corporate officers. In Alaska, we had taken a cable car to the top of a glacial mountain, and there, in a lodge with immense windows overlooking miles of mountains, Seward Bay, and hang gliders suspended against the ten o'clock sunset, we had toasted the Volvo corporate personnel, who had risen to ovations from the journalists, and made short witty speeches about how happy they were to have us there, and how important we were to them.

At the pre-dinner cocktail hour in Phoenix, caterers in black bowties brought around margaritas on trays, and bartenders served up the best of the top shelf. Some of the journalists arrived in jacket and tie. They clearly saw this occasion as a real event. While we picked hors d'oeuvres off a long oak table, I tried to do some research, to crack open something big, and to that end, I cornered Jim Borsh, Volvo's director of corporate communications.

A tall, serious man, Borsh had been on the Taliesin tour with me, and had not cracked a smile or told one joke, which was unusual for someone in public relations.

As we sipped margaritas and smacked the salt off our lips, he surprised me by saying that Volvo didn't expect to sell many C70s. The car was just part of a vast campaign to change Volvo's image. With its "sensual lines" and "supple skin," as the press release called them, the

C70 would sexify the stodgy automaker, making people feel better about buying Volvo sedans and station wagons. The success of the campaign, it was natural to infer, would depend on the articles we writers would write.

The next day, I packed up my sunglasses, lotion, windbreaker, pen, pad and pre-weathered baseball hat, and went home. I didn't really want to leave, but I had to. I bumped into Ree Hartwell on the front stoop of the hotel. As I mentioned, she is Volvo's media relations manager, and in that capacity was responsible not only for my happiness, but for choosing which journalists to invite on the press trips. As cynical as I was about the quid pro quo implicit in these junkets, I couldn't bring myself to announce it openly, so when she asked me if I had written anything about the Volvos I drove in Alaska, I equivocated.

"I'm not quite sure what I'm going to do with that," I said, sheepishly. Actually, I had never intended to write about it at all. I had told her that when she had invited me, but I still felt a twinge of guilt. Even though it was acknowledged by all parties that there was no pressure, we have all been trained from birth that if someone does something nice for you, you owe them one. "I think I might do something about this trip, though," I added, with more enthusiasm. And then, with the other writers, I stepped into the minivan which took us to the airport. I knew the trip was over when, waiting for my plane, I had to buy my own can of soda.

The Payoff

Based on an examination of some of the articles produced by the writers collaborating in Volvo's marketing plan, I've concluded that the amount it cost to send each journalist to Phoenix and back, in first-class accommodations, was more than paid for by the coverage Volvo received, especially when one considers that a full-page ad in a major magazine can cost up to and sometimes over ten thousand dollars. Volvo, along with other car manufacturers, has clearly concluded the same thing.

Not long after the trip to Alaska, for instance, I came across an article in *Bikini*. The author, in a story touted on the cover, raved about the XC wagon, and his article ran alongside a full-page photograph of him standing in front of the car. You can't buy coverage like that, Volvo knows, but you can barter for it. It reaches exactly the kind of audience Volvo

is trying for: younger, "hipper," more style-conscious buyers who might otherwise dismiss the Swedish carmaker as too square.

Another writer, in *The Detroit News*, not only regurgitated the press release's claim that the XC "looks as good at the Ski Haus as it does at the Opera House" but supplemented it with his own riff, adding that "the wagon did indeed blend in equally well at the Grouse Ridge Shooting Grounds, the banks of the Little Susitna River and the classy Alyeska Prince Hotel."

The Arizona trip bore fruit as well. A search on the Dow Jones network for mentions of "C70 Convertible" turned up four hundred forty articles. It would be impossible and, I fear, fatally tedious, to read every one. The hundred or so pages I could get through were scarily alike. Clearly Volvo had gotten their money's worth. I recognized the names of many of the writers. Some mentioned that they had been flown out to Phoenix or Alaska, and some wrote the review without mentioning their trip. Some simply lapped up what Volvo fed them, quoting directly from Diaz de la Vega and the slobbering press material.

New Car Test Drive, a publication available both on and off the Web, pretty much grabbed the first line of Volvo's press release to use as a headline, taking "The winds of change are blowing throughout Volvo" and changing it to "The winds of change are blowing here."

More subtle was the adoption of Volvo-fed words, like "swoop," which Volvo used in its press release and which at least two writers co-opted

for their own description of the car. One syndicated author actually sunk so low as to use the Volvo catch line, "Tan Safely," as his first sentence. His piece appeared in *The Automotive News* and, through syndication, in papers like *The Toronto Sun*.

A number of writers busted out a little ersatz erudition, pointing out that the C70 was not Volvo's first attempt at an open car, and mentioned the 1956 P1900, which, of course, had been helpfully parked outside the hotel. *GQ*'s writer, for one, penned a worshipful half-page about the C70, pretty much scooping up the press material and ladling it into his story, talking about the P1900 and adding some filigree about how much he'd like to have Ursula Andress in the car with him. The excitement offered to *GQ*'s half-million or so affluent readers might have paid for the whole American lifestyle wave.

Honorable mention for the most obsequious coverage should also be awarded to the *Autoweek* writer who added a nice bit of characterization to his transcription of Diaz de la Vega's speech, writing, "But what about taste? Diaz de la Vega gets a devilish glint in his eyes: 'A taste of the good life,' he says."

The highest honor in this category, however, should go to the online magazine *Woman Motorist*, whose author took Diaz de la Vega's speech in the Palmera Lounge as the outline for her entire review and ended her piece with the treacly, "Thanks, Volvo, for sensing everything today's driver needs."

5:30 P.M.—Friday

Cold wind and cars
stall in lines
on N. Lamar.
The parking lot to the
"natural foods" grocery store
and the "locally owned" bookstore
crowds with machines that complete
the escape from ignored
old earth-bound time
questioned by carbon dioxide
leaked in a moment to obtain
a six-pack of English beer.

Doppio

Latin beans
through Italian machines
for that perfect cup.
German autos in the parking lot
and Vivaldi in the coffee shop
drive the cost of comfort up
several cents per pound.

—Dale Smith

from
In The Country of the Young

THOMAS BEER

HUGH found that his mother did not like his pictures. She scolded him for wasting paper and chewing pencils. His twin sisters merely giggled when he brought them views of things familiar or sometimes seized him for a game. They wanted to dress him up and Mrs. Cullom never interfered with this hideous diversion. Unless his father or brother Ian effected a rescue, Hugh might be dragged to the attic and there robed in something sure to be uncomfortable and female. Ian was more gracious to Hugh's art. He would look at the last effort, nod gravely and say that it was pretty good never inquiring the subject. Hugh really preferred this calm to Aunt Kate Bartlett's laughing rapture or Uncle Henry's loud delight.

Grandmother Wells was the great impediment. She had no patience with pictures at all. She was likely to interrupt with shrill orders about washing or the learning of her catechism. Hugh was safe from this terrible woman only in the library. Into that still room she never came. The sills of the library doors somehow held her away. Elsewhere she raged incessantly, harrying hired girls. Farmhands recoiled from her,

coming into hasty employments. She invaded the garden and yelped at the witless flowers. But the square library walled in books seemed to repel her slow feet save when Hugh's father was in his office in town. Then, she might come down on Hugh comfortably at work under the broad table or send his sisters to pull him into the tumult of the red sitting room.

But when Mr. Cullom sat reading the library must be silent. Hugh could take refuge under the table unquestioned. A regiment of sharp pencils lay in a blue china dish beside the cigar box and his father did not care how many points Hugh broke. If Hugh panted aloud in the passion of art Cullom would reach out a slipper and prod him back into silence. But in his long shadow or behind the whirling bookcase, Hugh was safe. Mrs. Cullom couldn't remove him. Her skirts would flutter up to the table and voice would break out.

"Come, Hughie, Mrs. Brundred's fetched Florrie over to play."

"No," said Hugh.

"Now, come."

Then Cullom would say, "Oh, let him alone, Milly. He's happy."

"But Gus, Mrs. Brundred's fetched little Florrie over—"

"Let him alone."

Then the skirts fluttered off again, over the green matting to the red rug of the sitting room. Gratefully, Hugh would pat the long leg nearest. Sometimes Cullom chuckled. Usually he made no sign. The leaves of his book flapped. Hugh found that the leaves flapped most briskly when Grandmother Wells veered toward the sitting room sill. Hugh watched her yellow face turn to see his father and stared blandly at her crooked, summoning finger.

It was a surprise when he was lifted up on the shoulder of Uncle Henry's black coat and told to look down at the yellow face with its eyes tight shut. Her coffin lay among flowers by the library fireplace. Hugh wondered at her intrusion but wanted a white rose from the crust of white bloom on the sober cloth. He asked why she didn't speak.

"She's dead, son," said Uncle Henry.

Hugh wriggled. Death was a state overtaking cherished cats. He still wanted the white rose. The garden was deep in snow.

"Can't she talk, now?"

"No, sonny."

"Oh, my!" Hugh sighed out his happiness. He bent and stole a rose. Then, in the crowd of dark people someone laughed like his father. Lovely Aunt Kate carried Hugh off. A black veil covered her bright head but under it she smiled. In the upper hall the shutters were closed but light ran through the cracks and fell on the head of Ian chewing gum by the windows. This sun made his hair dance and glitter and soon music mixed with the light. Hugh seemed to swell with joy. He laughed wildly.

"Sh-sh!" said Aunt Kate.

"Oh, look at Janny's hair, Kate! Oh—"

"Yes, but hush, lover."

Ian sneezed and got out of the sun rays. Hugh played with the rose and listened to the music. Then, there was motion below. His mother cried on the stair and Cullom stood on the red landing, wonderful in his silk hat, talking against her sobs. ". . . None of them. I won't have any of them go to the cemetery."

"Gus is right, Milly," said Aunt Kate, "they're too young."

Carrie and Lucy yelled that they wanted to go to the cemetery but their parents vanished along with Kate and Henry. Ian threw the windows wide. A line of black carriages rolled down the drive to the lane where pools had the sheen of new tin. Nettie the hired girl and Somers the jolly, youngest farmhand came to open all the windows. The twins wept tiresomely. Ian took Hugh off to the barns where they found a strange tomcat who strutted about with his tail lustrously swaying and who grew dear directly.

"Oh, what's his name, Janny?"

"Dunno, bud. We'll ask papa."

Cullom always knew cats' names on sight. It turned out that this cat's name was Jonadab when he was brought to the house the next day.

"Now, Gus," said Mrs. Cullom, "that's a Bible name."

Ian observed, "I know who he was. Jonadab was the feller told that feller Amnon to—"

"Oh, Janny," Mrs. Cullom cried

out, "that ain't a nice part of the Bible!"

"You could say that about hunks of the Bible," said Uncle Henry.

Mr. Cullom stood looking curiously at Ian with his black eyes half shut for a moment, then he laughed, "Good lord, Janny remembered something!" He picked Ian up and set him afoot on top of the whirling book case. Ian smiled solemnly down at them all. A wish rose in Hugh's head. He wanted something.

"Oh, stick your leg out, Janny! Stick your leg out!"

"What for, bud?"

"Oh, O please, Janny! Your leg an' your arm!"

"I see," said Cullom, "it's the Mercury over at your house, Henry."

And with a leg and arm balanced, Ian did look like the naked bronze lad on Kate's piano. Hugh laughed and hugged Jonadab until the new cat wailed and escaped to the kitchen.

Jonadab was a tranquil, friendly beast who liked to sit watching Hugh make pictures. He graciously slept on the dresser in the blue room where Hugh lived with Ian at night. Hugh doted on Jonadab above all other cats since his friend got on excellently with Benjy the dog. But Jonadab died in May. He was buried in a soap box at the edge of the flowering apple orchard. Ian found a thick chunk of clean wood to mark the grave and on this Cullom carved letters that Ian read to Hugh, "Jonadab. A subtil man."

"Oh Gus," said Mrs. Cullom, "out of the Bible!"

"Well, why not? Jonadab wasn't any saint."

"It just don't seem right."

"Rubbish, Milly," said Cullom and gave Ian the headstone of Jonadab for whom Hugh did honorable mourning. Jonadab's destiny troubled him. God had taken

Jonadab. This God collected dead persons who then lived with him in remote comfort above the blue sky. Grandmother Wells, though, disliked cats. She berated their approach and counseled their destruction.

"And I guess God'd be scared of her," Hugh told his mother.

This was a mistake. Mrs. Cullom slapped Hugh then set out to tell him about God. Once she took him to a place of torment called Sunday School in town. Here several girls kissed him and Hugh saw his sisters in prim glory giggling together far from the circle of woe where he sat. But when he came home Cullom had arrived from Cleveland and spoke loudly to Mrs. Cullom so that she wept. As always, the girls wept too. Hugh ran off through the slope of woods with Ian to Aunt Kate's house where no one ever wept and maple sugar was to be had on application of kisses to the goddess. His dear aunt assured Hugh that God had made the world in six days, a fearful chore, and Hugh fancied his mother might like a picture of this.

On his sixth birthday, in June, he undertook the picture when Mrs. Cullom and the girls had gone proudly to church, in the new carriage. Nettie the hired girl gave Hugh a vast sheet of paper, slightly stained from beef but smooth and shiny. he considered the porch as a workroom, then disliked the heat and an intrusive young collie so sprawled on top of the marble table in the sitting room. Its coolness rose gloriously through his linen shell. Inspirations came fast. Ecstasy rent Hugh. He hummed.

"Here," said Cullom, in the library, "you sound like a steam whistle, buddy."

Hugh was silent but wrought on. Mighty thoughts circled his brain. Soon Ian trotted in from a swim, his hair darkened by water, and stood looking.

"It's God makin' the world," Hugh explained.

"Oh. Well, what's that he's got in his hand?"

"That's a saw. Other's a hammer."

Ian nodded and shuffled his pink bare feet on the red carpet. He said, "M, it's pretty good, bub, but I wouldn't let mamma see it."

Hugh doubted the advice, for once and in spite of Ian's general wisdom. A picture of God was surely designed to please Mrs. Cullom. His father came to look and laughed, kissing his ear.

"You're all right, brother Hugh."

Hugh chewed some cedar from his pencil. People called him anything: Son, sonny, bub, bud, buddy, brother Hugh, Hughie, lover, and sometimes Somers the farmhand called him kid. Had he any actual name? Oh, curious world! He began an elephant, recalling Ian's geography. The convenient structure of elephants was charming. He panted, effecting the trunk. Time passed. Presently, Mrs. Cullom drove in from church bringing ladies and Dr. Reece, the black-clad rector. Cullom groaned as Hugh crawled under the library table and made his queer, unmeaning remark of "Thus we find and so we see" then went in his long, slow steps to meet the light skirts and the rector's neat trousers. The voices rose to a squealing that meant pleasure. The ladies laughed before his father spoke. Hugh peeped, noting Mrs. Reece, a round woman who smelled of carnations and who always called Hugh "Sweetheart." She saw him and now his sisters came trotting to bring Hugh out.

"And what's this picture?" Mrs. Reece smiled, "Isn't it pretty? And tell me what it is, dear."

"It's God makin' the world," said Hugh.

At once all the voices stopped, then with a swift change to clatter, Hugh was floating upstairs, his mother's hand locked on his wrist. She wept. His sisters wagged their yellow braids and watched Hugh spanked. He was too frightened to cry and could only gasp at the closed door when Mrs. Cullom tossed him into the bedroom where Ian was pulling on stockings. Hugh bumped on the gray floor.

"I told you so," Ian said, but kindly, and poured some water from their jug on the oilcloth mat by the washstand. He picked Hugh up and sat him down in the cooling pool. The water soaked through Hugh's thin breeches and soothed him. He gazed at great Ian with awe for such sapience. Ian was never spanked, yet could devise remedies against spanking. Now he stood buttoning a fresh shirt over the rose of his chest so deftly that Hugh marveled. Not a button went amiss. Hugh adored Ian until the girls came twittering to say that he was to have no dinner. Hugh howled. Ian comforted him with a string of limp licorice before going downstairs. It seemed that the girls reported the spilt water, for Hugh heard his mother's voice just as a totally new, brindle cat walked down the oak branch and hopped on to the window sill. Hugh was stroking him when Mrs. Cullom dashed in, red faced.

"Oh, you bad, bad boy, Hugh Cullom! Spillin' water on the floor!"

Hugh cowered. His mother babbled incomprehensibly, her hands on her moving breasts. But Cullom came into the white doorway, a napkin spread over his arm and stood listening, then spoke with a jar of the voice that halted Hugh's breath, "Milly, I'm sick of this. You asked these dam' cattle here to eat. Go down and talk to them."

He towered. Hugh had never seen anyone so tall. The black head seemed to touch the white top of the doorway. Mrs. Cullom let her hands fall. The hair swayed above her face from which the red vanished.

"Oh, Gus," she said, "Gus!"

"Go downstairs."

Somehow she wilted from Hugh's sight. He stood staring at his father whose lashes drooped now and hid the flash of his eyes. The cat yawned on the window sill and clawed Hugh's wrist. Hugh thought suddenly that this cat's name was unknown to him. He scooped the creature in his arms and hurried to Cullom.

"Son," said the tall man, "you ought to know by this time that God's a piece of your mamma's personal property."

"Yessir. Papa, what's his name?"

Cullom recognized the cat at once. "That's Hamilcar Barca, bud. Go down tell Nettie to give you your dinner."

Hugh took Hamilcar Barca down the backstairs into the hot kitchen where Nettie was sitting on Somers' lap and feeding that entertaining farmhand chicken. She graciously abandoned him for Hugh, however, gave Hamilcar some melted ice cream and soon the kitchen was gay. Hugh admired Nettie as an accomplished woman. She could talk Swedish and balance a bone hairpin on her freckled nose. Somers played the jewsharp exquisitely, far better than Ian, Hugh admitted. Hugh felt giddy with pleasure while he ate chocolate cake in Nettie's lap, listening to Somers who played "Marching through Georgia." But the bell rang and when Nettie came scowling back from the dining room she bade Hugh be still, for, "Such a temper your mamma's got to her! I never!"

Somers put away the jewsharp and asked if it wasn't kind of dangerous. But Hugh thought of another spanking and fled with Hamilcar to the hayloft of the cowbarn. Here all was yellow peace. Hamilcar slew a mouse in the hay and civilly took it elsewhere. Hugh digested his dinner and watched the other hired men roll dice in the gray shade of the red ice house. From the loft's double door their bent bodies looked like blue cabbages of the kitchen garden, swelled and transplanted to the brown barnyard clay. They mentioned God and Christ ceaselessly. Hugh sighed over the behavior of women. Then Ian climbed up through the trap door and spoke gravely, "Mamma's sick. They got a doctor. She fell down on the floor. I guess she's awful sick."

"My," said Hugh hopefully. His memory of Grandmother Wells' departure was fresh and pleasing with its music and white flowers and rattling black carriages. Let his mother die, by all means. Perhaps Ian could arrange it, "Mebbe she'll die, Janny?"

The New Global Vulgate

PIERRE BOURDIEU AND LOÏC WACQUANT

CROSS the world, all manner of intellectual professions and state elites are speaking a strange new language whose vocabulary seems to have come from nowhere but is suddenly in everyone's mouths: "globalization" and "flexibility," "multiculturalism" and "communitarianism," "ghetto" and "underclass," and their so-called postmodern cousins: identity, minority, ethnicity, hybridity, fragmentation, and the like. The spread of this new global vulgate is the product and trace of a novel kind of academically based imperialism whose effects are all the more pernicious for being promoted by cultural producers who more often than not think of themselves as progressives.

Cultural imperialism rests on the power to cause particularisms linked to a singular historical tradition to be misrecognized as such. Just as in the nineteenth century a number of philosophical questions debated as universal throughout Europe and beyond actually originated in the historical particularities of the singular universe of German academics, as historian Fritz Ringer showed in his classic study

The Decline of the Mandarins,[1] so today a number of questions arising directly from intellectual confrontations over the peculiarities of American society and its universities have been imposed, in oddly dehistoricized form, upon the whole planet. These new commonplaces, in the Aristotelian sense of presuppositions of discussion that themselves remain undiscussed, owe much of their power to the fact that, circulating from academic conferences to best-selling books, from semischolarly journals to experts' evaluations, from commission reports to magazine covers, they are present everywhere at the same time, from Berlin to Tokyo and from Milan to Managua, and are powerfully supported and relayed through the allegedly neutral channels of international organizations (such as the OECD, the World Bank, or the European Commission) and public policy think tanks (such as the Manhattan Institute in New York City, the Adam Smith Institute in London, and the Saint-Simon Foundation in Paris).[2] Along the way, these commonplaces of the new global vulgate are transformed into a kind of universal common sense, leaving behind their

This is an adapted and shortened translation of "Sur les ruses de la raison impérialiste," which appeared in *Actes de la recherche en sciences sociales*, 121–122. Translated by Loïc Wacquant.

roots in the complex and controversial realities of a particular historical society—the United States of the post-Fordist and post-Keynesian era of "small government" and of the "compassionate capitalism" that is embraced by both Democrats and Republicans, now tacitly elevated to the rank of yardstick for all things and model for all nations. (It bears stressing to avoid any misunderstanding—and to ward off the predictable accusation of "anti-Americanism"—that nothing is more universal than the pretension to the universal or, more accurately, to the universalization of a particular vision of the world; and that the demonstration sketched here would hold, *mutatis mutandis*, for other fields and other countries at other epochs, including France.[3])

Of the distinctly American cultural products now being diffused on a planetary scale, the most insidious are not the apparently systematic theories (such as "the end of history" or "globalization") and pseudo-philosophical worldviews ("postmodernism"), as these are quite easy to spot. Rather, they are those isolated and seemingly technical terms such as "flexibility" or "employability," which, because they encapsulate and communicate a whole philosophy of the individual and of social organization and yet

seem so eminently practical, are able to function as political code words and mottoes—in this case, the downsizing and denigration of the state, the reduction of social protection, and the acceptance of casual and precarious labor as a fate, nay a boon.

Thanks to a symbolic inversion based on the naturalization of the schemata of neoliberal thought, whose dominance has been imposed for some twenty years by the relentless sapping of conservative think tanks and of their allies in the political and journalistic fields,[4] the refashioning of social relations and cultural practices in advanced societies after the U.S. pattern—founded on the pauperization of the state, the commodification of public goods, and the generalization of social insecurity—is nowadays accepted with resignation as the inevitable outcome of the evolution of nations, when it is not celebrated with a sheepish enthusiasm eerily reminiscent of the infatuation for America that the Marshall Plan aroused in a devastated Europe half a century ago.[5]

A number of related themes recently arrived on the European intellectual scene, and especially on the Parisian scene, have thus crossed the Atlantic in broad daylight or have been smuggled in under cover of the revived influence of the products of American research. Consider "political correctness," which is used, even more so in French intellectual circles than in America, as an instrument to suppress every subversive impulse, especially feminist or gay; or the moral panic over the "ghettoization" of so-called "immigrant" neighborhoods; or the moralism that insinuates itself everywhere and leads to a kind of principled depoliticization of social problems, stripped of any reference to domination (as exemplified by debates around the family but seeping into issues of crime and work); or, finally, the opposition between "modernism" and "postmodernism," which has become so canonical in those regions of the intellectual field closest to cultural journalism and which, founded as it is on an eclectic, syncretic, usually dehistoricized, and always highly approximate rereading of a platoon of French and German authors, is in the process of being imposed in its American form upon the Europeans themselves.[6]

In the debate swirling around "race" and identity the new global vulgate has brought similar, if more brutal, ethnocentric intrusions. A very particular historical representation—born from the fact that the American tradition superimposes on an infinitely more complex social reality a rigid dichotomy between whites and blacks—can even be foisted on countries where the operative principles of vision and division of ethnic differences, codified or practical, are quite different and which, in the case of Brazil, were until recently considered counterexamples to the "American model."[7] Carried out by Americans and by Latin Americans trained in the United States, most of the recent research on ethnoracial inequality in Brazil strives to prove that, contrary to the image that Bra-

zilians have of their own nation, the country of the "three sad races" (indigenous peoples, blacks descended from slaves, and whites issued from colonization and from the waves of European immigration) is no less "racist" than others, and that Brazilian "whites" have nothing to envy their North American cousins on this score. Worse yet, Brazilian *racismo mascarado* should by definition be regarded as more malign precisely on account of its being veiled and denegated. This is the claim of political scientist Michael Hanchard in *Orpheus and Power*: By applying North American racial categories to the Brazilian situation, Hanchard seeks to make the very particular history of the U.S. civil rights movement into the universal standard for the struggle of all groups oppressed on grounds of color (or caste).[8] Instead of dissecting the constitution of the Brazilian ethnoracial order according to its own logic, such inquiries are most often content to replace wholesale the Brazilian national myth of "racial democracy" (as expressed, for instance, in the works of Gilberto Freyre[9]) with the American myth according to which all societies are "racist," including those within which "race" relations seem at first sight to be far less hostile than the American model. In works like these the concept of racism no longer serves as an analytic tool but rather as a mere instrument of accusation; under the guise of science, it is the logic of the trial which asserts itself (and which ensures book sales).[10]

In a classic article published thirty years ago, the anthropologist

Charles Wagley showed that the conception of "race" in the Americas admits of several definitions according to the varying significance granted to descent, physical appearance, and sociocultural status (occupation, income, education, region of origin, and so forth) depending on the history of intergroup relations and conflicts in the different geographic zones.[11] The United States is utterly alone in defining "race" strictly on the basis of descent, and then does so only in the case of African-Americans: one is "black" in Chicago, Los Angeles, or Atlanta, not by the color of one's skin but for having one or more ancestors identified as blacks, that is to say, at the end of the regression, as slaves. The United States is the only modern society to apply the "one-drop rule" and the principle of "hypodescent," according to which the children of a mixed union find themselves automatically assigned to the "inferior" group—here the blacks, and only them.

In Brazil, on the other hand, racial identity is defined by reference to a continuum of "color," that is, by use of a flexible or fuzzy principle that, taking account of physical traits such as skin tone, the texture of hair, the shape of lips and nose, and of class position (notably income and education, as indicated by the well-known Brazilian saying "money whitens") generates a large number of intermediate and partly overlapping categories (more than a hundred of them were recorded by the 1980 census) and does not entail radical ostracism or stigmatization without recourse or remedy. Evidence for this is provided by statistics on segregation in Brazilian cities, which is strikingly less pronounced than in U.S. metropolitan areas, and the virtual absence of two typically U.S. forms of ethnoracial violence: lynching (another name for ritual caste murder) and urban rioting.[12] Quite the opposite in the United States, where there exists no socially and legally recognized category of "métis" (mixed-race).[13] In this case we are faced with a division that is closer to that between absolutely defined and delimited castes (proof is the exceptionally low rate of intermarriage: Fewer than 2 percent of African-American women contract "mixed" unions, as against about half of American women of Latino or Asian origin): a caste division that one strives to conceal by submerging it within the universe of existing ethnoracial orders as "revisioned" through U.S. lenses by means of "globalization." (That this projection of the American folk vision of "race" onto Brazil is effected with the best intentions in the world by progressive American analysts, including African-Americans, and is generally met with acclaim and enthusiasm by leaders of the Afro-Brazilian movement only compounds the difficulty of detecting their paradoxical contribution to reinforcing

the symbolic mechanisms at the root of racial domination in both the United States and Brazil.)

For all the prestige and authority of the various products of the U.S. academy that serve to facilitate this "globalization" of American problems (and thereby verify the Americanocentric understanding of "globalization" as the Americanization of the Western world and, eventually, of the entire universe), none of them are sufficient by themselves to explain the ability of the U.S. worldview, scholarly or semischolarly, to impose itself as a universal point of view, especially when it comes to issues (such as "race") where the particularity of the U.S. situation is particularly flagrant and particularly far from exemplary. One would obviously need to invoke here also the driving role played by the major American philanthropic and research foundations in the diffusion of the U.S. racial doxa within the Brazilian academic field at the level of both representations and practices. Thus, the Rockefeller Foundation and similar organizations fund a program on "Race and Ethnicity" at the Federal University of Rio de Janeiro as well as the Center for Afro-Asiatic Studies at the Candido Mendes University (along with its journal *Estudos Afro-asiaticos*) so as to encourage exchanges of researchers and students. But the intellectual current flows in one direction only. And, as a condition for its aid, the Rockefeller Foundation requires that research teams meet U.S. affirmative action criteria, applying in yet another way the

uniquely American black/white dichotomy to a country where it is, to say the least, ill-suited.

Alongside the role of philanthropic foundations, we must also include the internationalization of academic publishing among the factors that have contributed to the diffusion of American thought in the social sciences. The growing integration of English-language academic book publishing, along with the erosion of the boundary between academic and trade publishing, has helped encourage the circulation of terms, themes, and tropes with strong (real or hoped) market appeal—which, in turn, owe their power of attraction simply to the very fact of their wide diffusion. For example, Basil Blackwell, the large half-commercial and half-academic publishing house, does not hesitate to impose titles on its authors that conform to the new planetary common sense. Such is the case with the collection of texts on new forms of urban poverty in Europe and America assembled in 1996 by the Italian sociologist Enzo Mingione: It was dressed up with the title *Urban Poverty and the Underclass* against the opinion and will of its editor and of several contributors since the entire book tends to demonstrate the vacuity of the notion of "underclass."[14] Faced with the manifest reticence of its authors, it is all too easy for Basil Blackwell to claim that an enticing title is the only way to avoid a high cover price which would kill the book in question. (Needless to say, it is hardly the only publishing house to prioritize the dictates of global merchandising over intellectual value.)

Thus do purely marketing decisions homogenize research and university teaching in accordance with fashions coming from America, sometimes even managing to fabricate outright "disciplines" like cultural studies, this mongrel domain born in England in the Seventies, which owes its international dissemination—if not the whole of its existence—to a successful publishing strategy. That this "discipline" does not exist in the French university and intellectual life, for example, did not prevent Routledge from publishing a compendium entitled *French Cultural Studies*, on the model of *British Cultural Studies* (there are also volumes of *German Cultural Studies* and *Italian Cultural Studies*). And one may forecast that, by virtue of the principle of ethnico-editorial parthenogenesis in fashion today, we shall soon find in bookstores a handbook of *French-Arab Cultural Studies* to match its cross-channel cousin, *Black British Cultural Studies*, which appeared in 1997 (but bets remain open as to whether Routledge will dare *German-Turkish Cultural Studies*).

The same trajectory can be seen in the international diffusion of faddish notions like "cyborg" or the true-false concept of "underclass," which, through the effects of transcontinental allodoxia, has been imported by those Old World sociologists most anxious to experience a second intellectual youth by surfing on the wave of popularity for "Made in America" concepts.[15] To summarize quickly, European researchers hear "class" and believe the term refers to a new position in the structure of urban social space, while their American colleagues, with very few exceptions, hear "under" and think of a mass of dangerous and immoral poor people in a resolutely Victorian and racistoid manner. Paul Peterson, a distinguished professor of political science at Harvard University and director of the Committee for Research on the Urban Underclass of the Social Science Research Council (financed yet again by the Rockefeller and Ford Foundations), left no grounds for uncertainty or ambiguity when he summarized approvingly the findings of a 1990 conference on the "underclass": "The suffix 'class' is the less interesting component of the word. Although it implies a relationship between two social groups, the terms of this relationship remain indeterminate without the addition of the more familiar word 'under.' 'Under' suggests something low, vile, passive, resigned, and at the same time, something shameful, dangerous, disruptive, dark, malignant, and even demonic. And, as well as these personal attributes, it implies the idea of submission, subordination, and wretchedness."[16]

In virtually every national intellectual field, researchers have come forth to take up the scholarly myth of the "underclass" and to reformu-

late in these alienated terms the question of the relations between poverty, immigration, and segregation in their own country. One loses count of the articles and works that purport to prove—or, what amounts almost to the same thing, to disprove—with admirable positivist diligence the existence of this group in such-and-such a society, town, or neighborhood, on the basis of empirical indicators often badly constructed and badly correlated among themselves.[17] To pose the question of whether there exists an "underclass" (a term that some French sociologists have not hesitated to translate as "sous-classe," perhaps foreshadowing the revival of the concept of "sous-hommes" or *Untermensch*) in London, Lyon, Leiden or Lisbon, is to suppose at the least, on one hand, that the term is endowed with minimal analytic consistency and, on the other, that such a group actually exists in the United States.[18] Unfortunately, though, the semijournalistic and semischolarly notion of "underclass" is as devoid of semantic coherence as it is of social existence. The incongruous populations that American researchers usually group under the term—welfare recipients and the long-term unemployed, unmarried mothers, single-parent families, rejects from the school system, criminals and gang members, drug addicts and the homeless, when they do not refer to all ghetto dwellers in bulk—are lumped together in this catch-all category for the simple reason that they are perceived as living denials of the "American dream" of individual success and universal opportunity.[19]

Upon closer scrutiny, the "underclass" turns out to be nothing but a fictional group, produced on paper by the classifying practices of those scholars, journalists, and related experts in the management of the (black urban) poor who share in the belief of its existence and have thereby brought renewed scientific legitimacy to the scholars and a politically and commercially profitable theme to the rest.[20] Inept and ill-fitting in the American case, when imported to Europe it makes even less sense. The agencies and methods for the government of misery are vastly different on the two sides of the Atlantic, not to mention the differences in ethnic divisions and their political status.[21] "Problem populations" are neither defined nor treated in the same manner in the different countries of the Old World as they are in the United States. Yet most extraordinary of all is the fact that, in keeping with a paradox that we already encountered with regard to other false concepts of the globalized vulgate, the notion of "underclass," which has come to us from America, was in fact born in Europe. The term was actually coined in the Sixties by the economist Gunnar Myrdal, who derived it from the Swedish *onderklass*. Myrdal's intention, ironically, was to describe the marginalization of the lower segments of the working class in rich countries in order to criticize the ideology of capitalist societies.[22] One can see here how profoundly the detour through America can transform an idea: From a structural concept aiming to question the dominant representation of society emerges a behavioral category actually designed to reinforce that representation by imputing to the "antisocial" conduct of the most disadvantaged the responsibility for their own dispossession. (The same process of inverted transmutation, whereby a notion, theory, or paradigm is reinvented into its opposite, has happened in greater magnitude to the work of Foucault on power and identity, which most American exegetes misread as an attack on reason, a theoretical vindication of "identity"—a notion he exploded—and an exemplar of "postmodernism," a label he famously derided thus shortly before his death: "What is it that they mean by postmodernity? *Je ne suis pas au courant*").

As for those in the United States who, often without realizing it, are engaged in this huge international cultural import-export business, they occupy for the most part dominated positions in the American field of power and even in the intellectual field. Just as the products of America's big cultural industry—such as jazz and rap, or the commonest food and clothing fashions, like jeans—owe part of their quasi-universal appeal to youth to the fact that they are produced and worn by subordinate minorities,[23] so the top-

ics of the new global vulgate no doubt derive a good measure of their symbolic efficacy from the fact that, supported by specialists from disciplines perceived to be marginal or subversive—such as cultural studies, minority studies, gay studies, or women's studies—they take on, in the eyes of writers from the former European colonies, for example, the allure of messages of liberation. Indeed, cultural imperialism, American or otherwise, never imposes itself more utterly than when it is served by progressive intellectuals—or intellectuals of color in the case of "race"—who would appear to be above suspicion of promoting the hegemonic interests of a country against which they wield the weapons of social critique. In this manner, an apparently rigorous and generous comparative analysis can, without its authors even realizing it, help universalize a problematic made by and for Americans.

The United States may well be an "exceptional" country, but its exceptionalism does not reside where the national sociodicy and social science agree in placing it, namely, in the fluidity of a social order that offers extraordinary opportunities for mobility (especially in comparison with the supposedly rigid social structures of the Old World). On the contrary, the most

rigorous comparative studies conclude that the United States does not fundamentally differ in this respect from other industrial nations, although the span of class inequality is notably wider in America.[24] If the

United States is truly different, in accordance with the old Tocquevillian theme untiringly renewed and updated, its exceptionalism lies in the rigid dualism of its racial division. A second, paradoxical exceptionalism

is its remarkable, newly minted capacity to project as universal that which is most particular to it while passing off as exceptional that which makes it most ordinary. 🐌

Notes

1. F. Ringer, *The Decline of the Mandarins* (Cambridge: Cambridge University Press, 1969).
2. Among the books that attest to this rampant McDonaldization of thought, one may cite the elitist jeremiad of Allan Bloom, *The Closing of the American Mind* (New York: Simon & Schuster, 1987), immediately translated into French by Julliard under the title *L'âme desarmée* ("The Disarmed Soul," 1987), and the angry pamphlet by the neoconservative Indian immigrant (and Reagan biographer) based at the Manhattan Institute, Dinesh D'Souza, *Illiberal Education: The Politics of Race and Sex on Campus* (New York: The Free Press, 1991) translated into French with the title *L'Education contre les libertés* ("Education against Freedom," Paris: Gallimard, Collection le Messager, 1993). One of the best ways to spot the works participating in this new intellectual doxa is the unusual speed with which they are translated and published abroad (especially in comparison with scientific works).
3. On France, cf. P. Bourdieu, "Deux impérialismes de l'universel" in C. Faure and T. Bishop, eds., *L'Amérique des Français* (Paris: Ed. François Bourin, 1992).
4. P. Grémion, *Preuves, une revue européenne à Paris* (Paris: Julliard, 1989); *Intelligence de l'anticommunisme: le Congrès pour la liberté de la culture à Paris* (Paris: Fayard, 1995); J. A. Smith, *The Idea Brokers: Think Tanks and the Rise of the New Policy Elite* (New York: The Free Press, 1991); Keith Dixon, *Les Evangelistes du Marche* (Paris: Editions Liber-Raison d'agir, 1998).
5. On "globalization" as an American project, see N. Fligstein, "Rhétorique et réalités de la 'mondialisation,'" *Actes de la recherche en sciences sociales* 119 (September 1997): 36–47; on the ambivalent fascination with America in the post-war period, L. Boltanski, "America, America . . . Le plan Marshall et l'importation du 'management,'" *Actes de la recherche en sciences sociales* 38 (1981): 19–41; and R. Kuisel, *Seducing the French: The Dilemma of Americanization* (Berkeley, Calif.: University of California Press, 1993).
6. This is not the only case where, by a paradox typical of symbolic domination, a number of topics that the United States exported and imposed around the world, beginning with Europe, have been borrowed from those who now receive them as the most advanced forms of theory.
7. According to the classical study of C. Degler, *Neither Black Nor White: Slavery and Race Relations*

in Brazil and the United States (Madison, Wisc.: University of Wisconsin Press, 1995, first published 1974).
8. M. Hanchard, *Orpheus and Power: The Movimento Negro de Rio de Janeiro and São Paulo, 1945–1988* (Princeton, N.J.: Princeton University Press, 1994). One will find a partial antidote to ethnocentric poison on this subject in the work of Anthony Marx, *Making Race and Nation: A Comparison of the United States, South Africa and Brazil* (Cambridge: Cambridge University Press, 1998), which demonstrates that racial divisions are closely linked to the political and ideological history of the country under consideration, each state creating in a sense the conception of "race" which suits it.
9. G. Freyre, *Maîtres et esclaves* (Paris: Gallimard, 1978).
10. How long will it be before we get a book entitled "Racist Brazil" patterned after the scientifically scandalous "Racist France" of a French sociologist more attentive to the expectations of the field of journalism than to the complexities of social reality [Ed: This is in reference to Michel Wieviorka, *La France raciste* (Paris: Editions du Seuil, 1993)]?
11. C. Wagley, "On the Concept of Social Race in the Americas," in D. B. Heath and R. N. Adams, eds., *Contemporary Cultures and Societies in Latin America* (New York: Random House, 1965), 531–545.
12. E. E. Telles, "Race, Class, and Space in Brazilian Cities," *International Journal of Urban and Regional Research* 19, no. 3 (September 1995): 395–406; and G. A. Reid, *Blacks and Whites in São Paulo, 1888–1988* (Madison, Wisc.: University of Wisconsin Press, 1992).
13. F. J. Davis, *Who is Black? One Nation's Rule* (University Park, Penn.: Pennsylvania State Press, 1991), and J. Williamson, *The New People: Miscegenation and Mulattoes in the United States* (New York: New York University Press, 1980).
14. E. Mingione, *Urban Poverty and the Underclass: A Reader* (Oxford: Basil Blackwell, 1996). This is not an isolated incident: As this article is going to press, the same publishing house is embroiled in a furious row with the urbanologists Ronald van Kempen and Peter Marcuse to try and get them to change the title of their joint work, *The Partitioned City*, into the more faddish and glitzy *Globalizing Cities*.
15. As John Westergaard already noted a few years back in his presidential address to the British Sociological Association ("About and Beyond the Underclass: Some Notes on the Influence of the Social Climate on British Sociology Today," *Sociology* 26, no. 4 (July-September 1992): 575–587).

16. C. Jencks and P. Peterson, eds., *The Urban Underclass* (Washington. D.C.: Brookings Institute, 1991), 3.

17. Just three examples among many: T. Rodant, "An Emerging Ethnic Underclass in the Netherlands? Some Empirical Evidence," *New Community* 19, no. 1 (October 1992): 129–141; J. Dangschat, "Concentration of Poverty in the Landscapes of 'Boomtown' Hamburg: The Creation of a New Urban Underclass?" *Urban Studies* 31, no. 77 (August 1994): 1133–1147; and C. T. Whelm, "Marginalization, Deprivation, and Fatalism in the Republic of Ireland: Class and Underclass Perpectives," *European Sociological Review* 12, no. 1 (May 1996): 33–51.

18. In taking considerable trouble to argue the obvious, namely, that the concept of "underclass" does not apply to French cities, Cyprien Avenel accepts and reinforces the preconceived idea according to which it *does* apply to urban reality in the United States ("La question de l'underclass des deux côtés de l'Atlantique," *Sociologie du travail* 39, no. 2, April 1997: 211–237).

19. N. Herpin, "L'underclass dans la sociologie américaine: exclusion sociale et pauvreté," *Revue française de sociologie* 34, no. 3 (July–September 1993): 421–439.

20. L. Wacquant, "L''underclass' urbaine dans l'imaginaire social et scientifique américain" in S. Paugam, ed., *L'exclusion: l'état des savoirs* (Paris: Editions La Découverte, 1996), 248–262.

21. These differences have deep historical roots, as attested by a comparative reading of the work of Giovanna Procacci and Michael Katz: G. Procacci, *Gouverner la misère: la question sociale en France, 1789–1848* (Paris: Editions du Seuil, 1993); and M. Katz, *In the Shadow of the Poorhouse: A History of Welfare in America* (New York: Basic Books, 1997).

22. G. Myrdal, *Challenge to Affluence* (New York: Pantheon, 1963).

23. R. Fantasia, "Everything and Nothing: The Meaning of Fast Food and Other American Cultural Goods in France," *The Tocqueville Review* 15, no. 7 (1994): 57–88.

24. Cf. notably R. Erikson and J. Goldthorpe, *The Constant Flux: A Study of Mobility in Industrial Societies* (Oxford: Clarendon Press, 1992); Erik Olin Wright arrives at the much same result with a notably different methodology in *Class Counts: Comparative Studies in Class Inequality* (Cambridge-Paris: Cambridge University Press—Editions de la Maison des sciences de l'homme, 1997); on the political determinants of the scale of inequalities in the United States and of their increase over the past two decades, C. Fischer et al., *Inequality by Design: Cracking the Bell Curve Myth* (Princeton, N.J.: Princeton University Press, 1996).

Scelzi

Hasime Elshani

Evans

SUJETS DIVERS

Lil' Ajil & Joly M.

Le Mule

Continued from page 12

cat perched on her head) everything is different. Haraway's techno-optimism holds obvious appeal for the industry: *Wired*, for example, understands her work as proving that the advent of cybernetics is finally making democratic free will possible, leading the way to a place where "everything is up for grabs, from who does the dishes to who frames the constitution."

The society-wide confusion of corporate-sponsored populism with liberation comes into high relief when we make a hard-right from the cyber-business press to the realm of high libertarian ideology. *Reason* magazine is formally dedicated to "free minds and free markets," but its most remarkable editorial achievement lies in a curious journalistic stunt performed over and over again by a capable cast of writers: Our patriotic American belief in the intelligence of the common people, also known as consumers, is made to collide violently with the nose of whoever is besieging this month's corporation-in-distress. Agency, that staple of the Routledge anthology, is transformed by *Reason* into the silver bullet of corporate defense. As it is used here, agency means we express ourselves perfectly well through the market, through consumer choice; it means that neither the government nor industry groups have any business protecting anybody from anything; best of all, it transforms those who criticize

industry into the worst sort of (you guessed it) snobs and elitists, tacitly believing that the public are a collection of agency-deprived fools.

Like the works of Herbert Gans, *Reason* seems never to come up in the monographs and anthologies of the cult-studs. And yet one feels that, if only to temper their endless bloody shirt-waving about the persecution they have endured at the hands of the book-burning right, cult-studs should somehow be required to take a peek beneath the publication's easter-egg colored covers. They will find there a militantly pro-corporate right that, like consumer society itself, has no problem with difference, lifestyle, and pleasure; that urges the destruction of cultural hierarchy in language as fervid as anything to appear between the covers of *Social Text*. There are even fairly exact parallels to the cult-stud argument. A recent *Reason* feature story by anthropologist Grant McCracken, for example, celebrates the "plenitude" of endless lifestyle diversity as "the signature gesture of our culture." After chewing out the usual right-wing culture warriors (Bennett, Buchanan, Robertson) and dropping the obligatory bomb on the Frankfurt School (Herbert Marcuse is also singled out for article-length punishment in the November 1998 issue), McCracken hails the rise of "difference, variety, and novelty" and counsels his colleagues on the right to forget about suppressing the Other and adjust themselves to the "inevitable." Declaring a democratic interest in even the oddest cultural novelties, McCracken informs his conservative colleagues, in a passage astonishingly reminiscent of Andrew Ross at his Saturday night worst, that

> Line dancing provides an interesting and dynamic site for the transformation of gender, class, outlook, and, yes, politics. It is on the dance floor that cultural categories and social rules are being reexamined and, sometimes, reinvented.

Of course, the only thing that makes sense out of this world of endless differentiation is "the great lingua franca" of "the marketplace." It is capitalism that is breaking "the stranglehold of hierarchies and elites," the "consumer culture" that "is a cause and a consequence of plenitude."

Other *Reason*ers cite the cult-studs explicitly when making the argument. Editor Nick Gillespie grounds his 1996 defense of the movie industry entirely in the populist reflex as an established principle of legitimate social science, citing prominent cult-stud Constance Penley (best known for her work on pornographic fanzines in which the *Star Trek* characters get it on) as the authority for this most hallowed of culturisms: "All viewers or consumers have 'agency': they *process* what they see or hear—they do not merely lap it up." Gillespie makes the elusive-audience point again and again, bringing in cult-stud Henry Jenkins for extra legitimacy, before moving on to the inevitable flip side: The

elitism of critics of the entertainment industry. These are figures who are said to believe that "viewers lack virtually any critical faculties or knowledge independent of what program producers feed them," that "the idiot box . . . turns viewers into idiots," that we are "robotic stooges," "trained dogs," "dumb receivers," "unwitting dupes." Not that they say any of this about us in public, mind you. These are simply *implied*, the obvious consequence of their "top-down conception of culture," their focus on "authorial intentions"—and the equally obvious and far more loathsome corollary, that "they know best," that "the viewer simply can't be trusted," that "regulation by the government" is in order.

Ah, but the market, the glorious, plenitude-permitting market, makes no such elitist presumptions. Not only does the market permit all the excellent examples of "resisting readers" that Gillespie finds so very dope (of course he cites *Mystery Science Theater 3000*), but in the land of pop culture, "as with all market-based exchanges, knowledge, value, and power . . . are dispersed." The robots mock a lousy movie, ergo the government must leave Microsoft alone. Q.E.D.[†]

The *Reason* argument is remarkably flexible for all its simplicity. After looking through back issues I found it deployed on behalf of the advertising industry (we aren't fooled 100 percent of the time, you know), the tobacco industry (people choose to smoke cigarettes, you

---

[†] A more recent example is Senior Editor Charles Paul Freund's June 1998 *Reason* essay in which the Frankfurters are dissed yet again and a "culture . . . indifferent to elites and divorced from taste hierarchies" is trumpeted one more time. Freund concludes by saluting the "Birmingham School" for having "at least gotten in the schoolhouse door. A little more homework, perhaps, and the scholars will arrive at the answer which the audience itself found long ago." Meaning, of course, the virtues of "marketplace culture," where people find "opportunities for the liberation and satisfaction of their senses and their intellect."

know), the gun industry (not all kids murder their classmates, you know), Barnes & Noble (people choose to go there, you know), Microsoft (choice incarnate, you know), and Jesse Ventura, whose election as governor of Minnesota gives our Mr. Gillespie an opportunity to explain his populism in historical detail, complete with passages about the affection felt by the good people of Minnesota toward corporations and this towering whopper, which comes up as an explanation of, well, just about everything: "at the end of the twentieth century, 'money power'—indeed,

power in general—is far more concentrated in government hands than in corporate ones."

The same logic is also commonplace much further to the right. While the luminous names of Haraway, hooks, Jenkins, Penley, and Ross (along with the joys of the dance floor) may be entirely unfamiliar to the fulminating Rush Limbaugh, their insistence on audience agency in the face of the culture conglomerates, as well as their faith in democracy through pop culture and in the essential elitism of those who criticize it are as friendly and familiar to him as the winning smile of Ollie North. Rush's version of the populist reflex comes across with particular vigor in his 1993 collection of witticisms, *See, I Told You So*, in which he refers to his own rise as an object lesson in the fundamental justice of markets, as in this rousing invocation of decentered power and audience agency: "Nobody put me in that [dominant] position— no network, no government program, no producer. You in the audience who have voluntarily tuned the dial to my voice—you alone—have caused my success." On the other side of the coin from the "magic of the marketplace," of course, are the high-handed, top-down, know-it-all regulators who want "to use this country as their grand laboratory experiment" and we the people "as their guinea pigs." But meddling liberals are just the tip of the hegemony iceberg: Even worse is the "sheer arrogance" of the elitists who believe that "people who listen to my show are just too stupid to tackle America's complicated problems."

It's not long before the Frankfurt School, this time in the person of Theodor Adorno, is wheeled in for its ritual thumping.

III.

For all the recent talk of cultural disintegration from one side, and of intolerance and persecution from the other, it is sometimes astonishing how much basic agreement lies beneath the stormy surface of the culture wars. However we may fight over appropriations for the NEA, educated people everywhere can agree on the perfidy of cultural elitism. And whether we simply ignore the world of business or actively extol the corporate order, we all agree that our newfound faith in active, intelligent audiences makes criticism of the market philosophically untenable. Taste has been annexed to politics in a manner that trivializes both, leaving us with an understanding of "democracy" that refers increasingly to matters of accurate demographic representation, to a certain republican humility before the wisdom of the people. That left and right have entered into a new consensus is further suggested by movies like *Pleasantville*, where a scarcely believable smugness about the liberated present arises phoenix-like from the ashes of the old, gray flannel smugness. It may be a consensus of masturbating moms rather than muffin-baking moms; of dreadlocked millionaires rather than horn-rimmed millionaires; of Kirk and Spock fisting rather than exploring new galaxies; of culture war rather than cold war, but it is as confident about the glories of life in these United States as any intellectual order has ever been.

If cultural studies has a unique intellectual virtue, it is a willingness to acknowledge its own failings, and in this essay I have made liberal use of the work of several of the discipline's most prominent critics. But in many other ways this new discipline looks, reads, behaves, and legitimates just like its never-acknowledged consensus forebears. For all the cult-studs' populist pretensions, the dominant tone of much of their writing is one of bombastic self-congratulation and vainglorious gasconade—sometimes self-pitying, sometimes pompous beyond belief. Even more indicative of the hardening of a new consensus is the cult-studs' strange fantasy of encirclement by Marxists at once crude and snobbish, a transplanted Cold War chimera that is rehearsed in just about every one of the discipline's texts, that leaps out from the jaunty Vaneigem quotes that fill the e-mail signature lines of the academically stylish.[†] The point here isn't merely that the right and the cult-studs use an identical target for bayonet practice, but simply that their target is a straw man, that the facts of American life are being ignored out of feigned anxiety over a cartoonish doctrine we imagine as both Teutonic and red, a horrifying cross between the nation's historical enemies. Business

---

† "People who talk about revolution and class struggle without referring explicitly to everyday life, without understanding what is subversive about love and what is positive in the refusal of constraint, have corpses in their mouths." Beginning in early 1997 this battle cry seemed to appear everywhere in cult-stud circles, even though Raoul Vaneigem evidently came up with its ringing cadences thirty years before. Its enthusiastic repeating across the cultural studies left betokens a weird belief that there are a great number of people in America who "talk about revolution and class struggle," and that these people need desperately to be defied.

publications are crowing these days that the production and export of culture are becoming the central element of the American economy; they see the millennium in the conquest of the world by Disney and Microsoft. But up on the heights from which critical fire might be brought to bear on the imperial parade, the self-proclaimed radicals are busy tying themselves in knots to avoid any taint of "master narratives."

Most revealing of all, though, is the cult-studs' marked complacency about their own role in the larger cultural economy. To be sure, this subject—the duties and responsibilites of intellectuals—is one they discuss frequently. Andrew Ross, for example, brilliantly dissects intellectuals' power to "designate what is legitimate" and to identify "what can then be governed and policed as illegitimate or inadequate or even deviant." But in Ross's telling the cult-studs themselves appear only as a solution to this historical problem. He does not consider what might happen when the ideas of legitimacy fancied by the corporate world change, when businessmen cease to care about high culture and talk instead about the wisdom of the audience and the power of the free-range entrepreneur. After leading readers through a century of snobs and aristocratic Trotskyists, Ross concludes his story of intellectuals and popular culture by locating himself and his colleagues in a place where such behavior by academics is no longer possible. He misses entirely the fatal irony of an academic radicalism becoming indistinguishable from management theory at exactly the moment when capitalist managers decided it was time to start referring to themselves as "radicals," to understand consumption itself as democracy.

In advertising agencies and market-research firms the gap between critical intellectuals and simple salesmanship shrinks and shrinks. With or without the assistance of the cult-studs, American audiences are growing more skeptical by the minute; fashion cycles that once required years now take months; heroes of the age like Bill Gates are despised in spite of the best efforts of his apotheosizers in the media. For business the intellectual task at hand is not so much legitimation as it is infiltration, and suddenly questions like the subversive potential of *The Simpsons* aren't as academic as they once seemed. Given the industry's new requirements, the active-audience faith of the cult-studs becomes less an article of radical belief and more a practical foundation for the reprioritized audience research being done by the new breed of corporate anthropologists, who move to the world of marketing directly from graduate school. One day they're studying the counterhegemonic funeral wailing of the Warao people, the next they're turning their attention on a nation of alienated 7-Eleven shoppers and hegemony-smashing mallwalkers. It's one of the glories of the age: a down-to- earth intelligentsia, focusing for once on our everday lives, speaking up for our agency, thoughtfully repositioning brands so as to help us defy confining social structures. Surely resistance is everywhere.

Zen and the Art of Self-Satisfaction

Julia Cameron, the principal author of **The Artist's Way: A Spiritual Path to Higher Creativity** (with Mark Bryan, Putnam, 223 pages, $13.95 paperback), claims "to tap into the higher power that connects human creativity with the creative energies of the universe." What she has really tapped into, though, is a pungent reservoir of the same old shit. *The Artist's Way* reads at times exactly like contemporary poetry, at other times like economic theory, and at still other times like a combination of management jargon, NPR commentary, and friendly academic feminist anthropology. There are several bleak moments in which *The Artist's Way* sounds like all of these, and like everything else as well, giving the reader the vertiginous sense that everything he has ever read has brought him to this book and there abandoned him. One finds oneself clutching the edges of the pages a bit too hard, as if to keep from pitching forward into the page and falling forever into a bottomless and eerily familiar abyss.

It is an abyss that has already swallowed a large number of people. Although *The Artist's Way* was originally marketed as "a spiritual path to higher creativity," a manual for aspiring artists, its appeal has proved far more general. The book's basic conceit—that everyone, deep down, is an artist—seems to have hit its mark: It's sold more than a million copies and inspired a cottage industry of sequels. Optimists might argue that *The Artist's Way* affords a glimpse of what the world will look like once high and low are collapsed for good and the

closed, hierarchical universe of art is finally opened to the healthful principles of democracy. It seems more honest, though, to find in it a glimpse of a world of universalized therapeutic nonsense, of banality in the service of social control and smug quiescence, a world hinted at by the title of one of the series' recent installments—*The Artist's Way at Work.*

The authors of *The Artist's Way* appear to be every bit as damaged as their prose. Julia Cameron, or "Little Julie" as she sometimes calls herself, is a recovering alcoholic, Martin Scorsese's ex-wife, and a one-time writer for *Rolling Stone*, in something like that order. Mark Bryan, who helped her write the book, is Cameron's former husband and is said to be an expert in "business creativity," which is probably all that needs to be said about him. Neither Cameron nor Bryan is an artist in the conventional sense, and this explains how they can be simultaneously uncomprehending of and condescending to art in all its forms.

Like most self-help gurus, Julia Cameron professes a very American belief in redemption through individual action, linking it, as always, to an even more American conviction that everyone needs desperately to be redeemed. We can all learn to be successful, she argues, because everyone is a failure to begin with. "[W]e are all creative," she tells us in one breath, and then in the next, "all of us are [blocked] to some extent." We all fail to live up to our full potential as artists, much as welfare mothers fail to live up to their potential as entrepreneurs. This is where the book comes in—job training, as it were, for the aesthetically underprivileged.

Like most job training programs, *The Artist's Way* teaches no actual skills. Cameron avoids making even the most basic suggestions about the mechanisms of art: Nowhere does she indicate, for instance, that painters should learn how to mix paint, or that violinists need to practice regularly, or that poets should, at least occasionally, read poetry. This is because Cameron doesn't think of art as a craft, or even as a hobby, but as a health issue. If you are not an artist, you are unwell; to become an artist therefore requires not practice, but convalescence and "recovery." Cameron does not want to teach, she wants to "daub and soothe and cool," and, in accordance with this desire, she has crafted a program based loosely on her own experience with Alcoholics Anonymous. Through twelve easy steps, blocked artists can recover a sense of "safety," "power," "abundance," a sense, in other words, that they have a rightful place at the center of the universe. This centrality is literal, not figurative: God himself is an artist, Cameron maintains, and "artists like other artists." With friends in such high places, one might think that artists were a pretty hardy group, but this is not the case. According to Cameron artists are barely held together by "self-nurturing" and self-pity. Spend quality time alone with your own "inner artist-child," Cameron says, or the little fella will curl up and die. Buy yourself "luxuries" like expensive perfume and "gold stick-'em stars" or your creativity will wither. Do what *you* want because "Artists cannot be held to anybody else's standards!" A good first act of self-assertion, Cameron suggests, might be dyeing your hair.

Given their frailty, it should come as no surprise that criticism is very dangerous to most artists. Some criticism, Cameron reluctantly admits, can be useful, but most is "artistic child abuse," and "all that can be done with abusive criticism is to heal from it." As damaging as criticism from others is, however, self-criticism is worse. The "Censor"—the part of the mind which criticizes artistic output—needs to be outwitted, and the way to do this is through the creation of "morning pages," a small batch of stream-of-consciousness writing to be done every morning for the rest of your life. Freewriting is, of course, a staple of high school English courses, and a well-established way for writers to generate ideas. For Cameron, though "morning pages" are not the beginning of the writing process; they are a metaphor for all artistic endeavor. Art comes out of people naturally and unreflectively, like urine. The artist should not think about his work; he should, as minor filmmaker Martin Ritt says, "*just do it.*" Cameron quotes Ritt several times in her book; she also quotes just about everyone else, from Oscar Wilde to Albert Einstein to Duke Ellington. She does not, however, quote Jonathan Swift, nor James Baldwin, nor Public Enemy, nor, for that matter, any other satirists or social critics. The reason is clear enough: For people like James Baldwin art is a form of thought, a way of engaging society by criticizing it, arguing with it, and challenging it. For Julia Cameron, on the other hand, art takes place in a pseudo-Zen emptiness outside of thought, outside of society.

Though Cameron's artists are free of all social connections, they are also rather helplessly bourgeois. Art does not pay very well, and its practitioners, therefore, tend to be people who can afford to be frivolous. Among those who have successfully used *The Artist's Way*, Cameron writes, are "Edwin, a miserable millionaire . . . Timothy, a . . . curmudgeon millionaire," and "Phyllis, a leggy, racehorse socialite." The purpose of *The Artist's Way*, in part, is to reassure Edwin, Timothy, and Phyllis that despite it all they are really very nice; indeed, they are enormously talented and wonderful. The reason that they feel miserable is not that they have built their lives on treachery, deceit, and callousness, but that they were unjustly "wounded" by parents, teachers, and friends who told them that they could not have absolutely everything they wanted. The reason that things come easily to them is not because they are rich, but because the universe is organized to benefit artistic people like themselves. "God is unlimited in supply and everyone has equal access. . . .

We deprive no one with our abundance," says Cameron.

Some might argue that all of this is beside the point. *The Artist's Way* is, after all, a self-help book, not a philosophical treatise. It does not claim to offer political insight: What it claims is that it will make us more creative, and that it will make us happy. Most people who pick up *The Artist's Way* want merely to know if it will help them, if it works. Many of us tend to forget that the list of things that work is long and not particularly glorious. Capitalism works. So does Western medicine, fascism, advertising, and polling. So does slavery.

Let me say in its defense, then, that *The Artist's Way* works, and that it will make you happy. Some day, I feel certain, it will work so well that, across the country, men and women everywhere will rise, write their morning pages, and spend the rest of the day brimming with creative energy. On that day, painters, writers, performance artists, and filmmakers will blissfully explore their childhood traumas and arrive at public healing strategies. Policemen will be filled with joy as they inventively and playfully beat a black man who has wandered into a gated community. Photographers will take rich, zesty pictures of anorexics, and publishers will think up exciting ways to convince female readers that they should look like those models. Lawyers heady with God-flow will brainstorm ways to legally drop people from the rolls of HMOs. But more than that, I see a day when the black man who is beaten doesn't mind, and the woman who starves herself doesn't mind, and the cancerous child without health insurance doesn't mind either. For they, too, will be cultivating their own creativity. The man will aesthetically modulate his screams and be happy. The woman will stick her fingers down her throat, vomit in an attractive pattern, and be happy. And the child's brain will be slowly, inevitably, and painlessly eaten away, as across his face spreads a comforting and meaningless smile.

—Noah Berlatsky

Smoke, Drink, Don't Think

When I was in grade school in the late Seventies, all the other girls used to get together during recess to talk about which Charlie's Angel they wanted to be. The überbabes tended to view themselves as Jills, flipping their hair back à la Farrah, while the submissive but popular ones were often Kellys. Even the ugly-duckling brainiacs had a place in the hierarchy, though admittedly they had to resign themselves to being Sabrinas. There was a clandestine air to the way these girls gathered in the cafeteria or the bathroom to discuss their roles, an exclusivity that was especially palpable for me since we didn't have a TV at my house. I was left out of the roundtables, and was once even accused of being a Bosley.

When I was at my place of employment in the late Nineties, all the other white-collar women used to pass around trade paperbacks. In the course of their lunchroom discussions they never mentioned which of the characters they wanted to be; gone were the open identifications of fourth grade. But there was something in their warm and collective appreciation of so-called "women's" fiction that was still alien to Bosleys like me. And of all the books they read in 1998, none was quite as extraterrestrial as Rebecca Wells's critically beloved bestseller **Divine Secrets of the Ya-Ya Sisterhood** (HarperCollins, 356 pages, $14.00 paperback).

This perky saga of a passel of debutante girlfriends growing up in Louisiana—the lovable, self-named Ya-Yas of the title—warmly recounts the fun they have playing together, praying together, and staying together from cradle to grave. Its plot hinges on the midlife crisis of one of their precocious but neurotic offspring, who directs a hit play, gets engaged, has an existential realization (death is mandatory), decides she doesn't "know how to love," goes off to find herself in a quaint woodsy cabin, and in the end marries Prince Charming as we always knew she would. At which point the angels pretty much commence to weep:

The angels attending her that night . . .
wanted to rock, they wanted to roll. . . .
They wanted to taste the saltiness of
tears the way Sidda did, the way Vivi did,
the way—if the truth be told—almost
everyone did on the night Sidda Walker
wed Connor McGill.

Now, critics and co-workers don't hail
Ya-Ya for being the most rigorously by-
the-numbers melodrama or most predictable series of clichés to appear in
years. No, they love the book because,
in its celebration of "female friendship,"
it's said to be confrontational, subversive, and yet reassuring. But what is
most striking about *Ya-Ya* is its simul-
taneous glorification of privilege and its
giggly   applause   for   women's
marginalization. It's hard to see it as
much more than a ruling-class Harle-
quin romance: The Ya-Yas are vapid,
pampered, self-obsessed Barbie dolls
who pass their time picnicking and
drinking highballs together. What common values they have beyond purchas-
ing power are neatly summarized by the
Billie Holiday *bon mot* that appears on
the very first page, "Smoke, drink, don't
think." Between the drinking and the
not thinking, they occasionally do their
bit for society by giving their Givenchy
coats as hand-me-downs to the black
maid. Meanwhile, their husbands are
largely invisible—off running the country, no doubt. After all, someone's got to
be doing the dirty work of Commerce and
State. What a giddy romp!

Furthermore, this author really
means it, we realize with a start. Here
is how Wells describes our heroine trotting out her "Yankee sweetheart" for the
approval of her Southern family: "She
could not stop smiling as she watched
her Yale-educated scenic designer release the Good Ole Boy within." This
mass-market paperback shorthand appears throughout the book, with "Yale-
educated" (elite-rich) and "Good Ole Boy"
(elite-white) serving to reassure us that
no matter what our differences—be we
descendants of slaveowners or Boston
Brahmins—we can always find bonho-
mie among the ranks of our class.

The repulsiveness of this fairly
simple point—rich people *can* have fun—
is magnified by the book's unforgivable
pretentiousness. Sporting an H.L.
Mencken epigraph, it seems to see itself
as symphonically profound, even transcendent. And yet, if I had a dollar for
every friend of mine who's waxed appre-
ciative of this feculent frolic, I'd be able
to run out and buy a Givenchy coat of
my own. Evidently intelligent women no
longer need to hear about equality or au-
tonomy; pseudo-intellectual celebrations
of female friendship are quite enough to
give their reading that pro-female patina.
(Let's not say *feminist*; the Ya-Yas
wouldn't. Such a strong, ugly word. Someone might misunderstand.) By throwing
in a few references to goddesses, the Virgin Mary, and the Moon, Wells brings off
a truly impressive insult to the sex.

To demonstrate its open-mindedness,
the book makes a few minor concessions
to identity politics. There's a gay costume designer who does "fabulous Diana
Ross imitations" and a black servant
who talks back. In a fit of grrrlish rebellion, the young Ya-Yas restore the original African stylings and copious makeup
to a Cuban statue of the Virgin that one
of their mothers has made them white-
wash. And once, in a rare and daring bit
of overt political commentary, George
Bush is mildly insulted. (On the other
hand, the child Ya-Yas sob nostalgically
for the Confederacy after viewing *Gone
With the Wind*.) But essentially this fable
exists to wax romantic and warm-hearted
about the sacrament of marriage. At the
story's climax, all but one of the now-eld-
erly Ya-Yas muster their feeble force and
travel en masse from the Bayou to Puget
Sound in a courageous campaign to convince our play-directing protagonist to
marry her fiancé. And the prospect that
the all-important nuptials might fall
through is the only thing, it turns out, that
will bring the remaining Ya-Ya—Sidda's
estranged and drunken mother, Vivi—to
forgive our heroine for gossiping about her,
thus arranging for a happy ending.

More insulting than the repetition of
tired formulae for female fulfillment,
however, is the host of aesthetic presumptions that inform this magnum
opus. *Ya-Ya* is genre fiction for the age
of demographics, targeting a well-heeled

readership with an oddly stilted idiom. Specifically, it is addressed to those liberated suburbanites who will not be confused or offended by, for example, this passage in which Sidda writes her affianced:

> Connor, unequaled—. . . My, but you gardeners know how to romance a blossom. Take my breath away, why don't you?

Or this description of her masturbating:

> So Sidda touched herself. She touched her blossom until, out of self-love, it swelled and quivered.

It's like *Designing Women* with a slightly less oblique vocabulary. There's also a clubby, precious feeling to much of the prose—euphemistic yet vulgar, repressed, and lurid at the same time; not self-scrutinizing, but often self-congratulatory; not strong, but very, very smug. Sentences, paragraphs, entire chapters with these attributes present a nicely balanced style equation, offering a perfectly circumscribed indulgence to the target reader—in this case a woman, who in *Ya-Ya* seems to be looking for assurances that she is both fallen from grace and upwardly mobile. She's both oppressed and leisured enough to enjoy it. After all, in the face of derision and bigotry from so many quarters, it's nice to know that those of us with a little family money can sit back, ignore the world, and paint our toenails together.

But let's say for a minute that this novel did, in fact, successfully celebrate female friendship instead of privilege and preening: In what way would that render it pro-female? Women haven't had the franchise for all that long, nor the right to education, to equal pay, or to run for office, and in most of the world they still don't; but what we most want to read about, apparently, is our ability to like each other. And to like ourselves.

The end of the book sees Sidda dancing happily on her wedding night and ready to start work on her second theatrical triumph (she will follow *Women on the Cusp* with *The Women: A Musical*). As the final line reads,

> For Siddalee Walker, the need to understand had passed. . . . All that was left was love and wonder.

Who needs to understand? Just cavort and compare cup sizes, ladies, and live happily ever after.

—Lydia Millet

The Prole Inside Me

Crime writer Jim Thompson spent his final years in Hollywood amid decidedly grim circumstances: None of his twenty-nine books remained in print, he was in ill health, and his talents were exploited by up and coming young Hollywood spoon-wearers. Shortly before he died in 1977, he is believed to have told his family to maintain all the rights to his fiction: "Just you wait! I'll be famous after I'm dead about ten years!" It could have been a moment from one of the astringent family melodramas he'd produced among his crime novels. Except, of course, that the decade or so following his demise proved the old man right. In 1983 Thompson's 1952 novel *The Killer Inside Me* was issued as a "Quill Mysterious Classic" amid a general revival of interest in Thompson and the violent, melodramatic fiction of his era. In 1984, three years after Geoffrey O'Brien published his survey *Hardboiled America*, Barry Gifford's Black Lizard Press began reprinting the rest of Thompson's oeuvre along with the forgotten works of other crime writers of the Forties and Fifties. After both *The Grifters* and *After Dark, My Sweet* appeared in theaters in 1990, Black Lizard was even absorbed into the formidable Vintage line of adult trade paperbacks.

At the same historical moment that this initial revival was finding a certain market success, the mavericks of academic postmodernism were admitting all manner of once-secondary literatures into the sacred canon of culture. Crime fiction was among the first and most widely noted in a slew of rediscovered splinters that would eventually include rock videos, sci-fi cults, pornography, and the collected works of navel-baring pop singers. Yet texts like Robin Winks's *Detective Fiction: A Collection of Critical Essays* (1988) and anthologies like Tony Hillerman's 680-page *Oxford Book of American Detective Stories* (1996) still conspicuously omitted the works of Thompson and his colleagues Chester Himes, David Goodis, and Charles Willeford. Thus Robert Polito's recent compilation of eleven writers in the two-volume Library of America anthology **Crime Novels: American Noir of the 1930s and 40s / 1950s** (990 pages, hardback / 892 pages, hardback) gives a peculiar final legitimacy and visibility to both the revivalist and postmodern thrusts. In it the works of forgotten novelists are pulled from oblivion's maw like so many black teeth and transformed into elegant, embossed, cloth hardbacks with ribbon markers, well-sewn bindings, and all the other accessories that a $35-per-volume price tag entails. Though Messrs. Goodis, Willeford, and Himes may never achieve the kind of stature among the ambitious young literati as, say, Chuck Bukowski, the Library of America anthology gives their erstwhile ten-cent paperback products the hushing gravity of permanence.

The Library of America volume also comes in the wake of a third canonization: These novels are now the ur-texts of the age of Tarantino, an instant tradition to sanctify Hollywood's newest ultranoir product lines. Like the B-pictures of the Forties and Fifties that were remade into a host of major-studio action films, these books are a trove of theme, prop, and gesture ready to be transformed into salable attitude. The novels work as pulpy confirmation of what we now know from *Pulp Fiction* (and the raft of pointless imitators—*Two Days in the Valley, Things to Do in Denver When You're Dead*—which still lurk like muggers on the video racks): the cinematic recombination of violence into irony, the nuanced terrors of intentional assault transformed into a snappy, empty contradiction, a meaningless rebus whose solution is "No, fuck *you*" (Bang!). The reader of today must make an imaginative portage around the post-Tarantino Niagara in order to see a history worth tracing: the ways in which these novelists, working under tight deadlines for short money, constructed a vision of their times wholly different from the ultranoir of today, where every scumbag is witty and the law never arrives. Read closely and their claustrophobic world still materializes; the quaintness one expects never shows up at all.

The crime fiction of our own day is different. Unlike the old paperbacks, the genre now rests on a bedrock of moral comfort that provides its readers—all their prurient enthusiasms notwithstanding—with reassuring references to their own carefully monitored public lives. In most contemporary detective stories (the works of Patricia Cornwell or James Patterson, for example) criminal action is approached from the comfort zone of outrage, understood as a ghastly, contemptible flouting of the forces of order. Most such novels—despite the badass boasting of their blurbs and glossy jackets—return to a fundamental affirmation of this wholesome, imagined social norm.

By contrast, the novels collected in the Library of America anthology, despite their diversity in date and style, only offer this sense of group propriety either as a savage narrative joke on a hapless character or as a thing to *be* savaged by an outwardly jovial but inwardly fractured man. Their jaundiced social vision, used to connect to a similarly alienated reader, makes these novels seem less a precursor of today's product and more a mutation of the proletarian literature of the Depression, which gained some prominence in the Thirties and Forties, but then dropped precipitously out of favor in the postwar period (a time, of course, when overt leftist expression in general took a hard fall down the station house staircase). Almost nobody talks about proletarian fiction today. Yesterday's transgression has a knack for reappearing as today's fashion, but for this genre, with its earnest Okies and utopian faiths, it seems unlikely that the marketing tricks that have made vintage crime so appealing to today's eager daddy-o's will work or even be tried.

The recent public enthusiasm for the tropes of noir obscures the commonalities between these schools. And yet so similar were the circumstances under which proletarian and crime writers emerged in the Thirties that any distinctions between what are obviously different sorts of novels become blurred upon close reading. Dashiell Hammett's *Red Harvest* (1929), for example, can be read

as a representative of both styles, with its "Continental op" (read Pinkerton) who shifts allegiances between a corrupt mining concern and the mob in the booming Montana company town of "Personville" (read Butte). Hammett describes potential social resistance but little comes of men's earnest efforts except for a large pile of bodies. Or consider the career of Jim Thompson, who joined the Wobblies as an itinerant oil worker in 1926, and then had a twenty-odd-year long "apprenticeship" writing for true-crime magazines and less respectable outlets like the *Los Angeles Mirror*. During this time, he wrote a number of openly leftist manuscripts, including a "hobo novel" and a nonfiction study based on his work with the Oklahoma Writers' Project, "We Talked About Labor," both of which were eventually scuttled. His debut novel, *Now and On Earth* (1942), a protracted portrait of a high-pressure bookkeeping job in a wartime aircraft plant populated by gung-ho rabble, merged a hellish take on family life with his gathering disillusionment with the proletarian cause. *The Killer Inside Me*, which remains arguably the most claustrophobic paperback

original ever, describes the life of a police officer who both enforces a town's cloying normality and indulges privately in all manner of sadistic pastimes (among other things, he extinguishes a cigar in the outstretched palm of a Thirties-style hobo).

James M. Cain's *The Postman Always Rings Twice* (1934), the first entry in Polito's anthology, is a compact tale that reminds us of the crime novel's origins in the Dreiserian overtness of proletarian narrative. Cain's narrator is as cynical about capitalism as one of Hammett's hard-boiled protagonists, but rather than an enforcer of bourgeois order he is a minor grifter adrift in Depression California, his station summarized by the book's opener: "They threw me off the hay truck around noon." Professing a yen for "the road," he only lingers in a cafe job to seduce the proprietor's sullen, bitter wife. While the narrator is laconic about his life circumstances, she simmers with a sexualized resentment (describing her life in California as "two years of guys pinching your leg and leaving nickel tips and asking how about a little party tonight") that somehow gets reconfigured as adul-

terous violence seasoned with purely proletarian economic reasoning: "And do you think I'm going to let you wear a smock, with Service Auto Parks printed on the back, Thank U Call Again, while he has four suits and a dozen silk shirts? Isn't that business half mine? Don't I cook? Don't I cook good? Don't you do your part?" Here the hard knocks of working-class life evolve into crime fiction archetype: The amoral woman, made sexually dominant by poverty, lures another archetype, the hapless and economically impotent male grifter, into criminal violence. Such themes are frequently adduced to characterize the mostly male genre of crime writing as misogynist hackwork; here, however, such misogyny might be better understood as a natural consequence of the grinding economic deprivation that reduces both men and women to quasi-pornographic components.

Although Cain is almost never recalled for the social consciousness of his crime fiction—or for his thoroughly redbaited 1946 attempt to form a writers' union—his debut bears comparison to that of proletarian writer Tom Kromer, whose sole completed novel, *Waiting for Nothing*, was published by Knopf in the same year as *Postman*. Kromer's book is a disjunctive, immediate narrative of life "on the stem": bargaining for green baloney butts, riding the rails, coupling with an amateur prostitute for warmth and a well-heeled homosexual for food. Although his narrator is chattier and more overwrought than Cain's bitter, calculating lovers, they all concur on the lack of space between personal circumstance and the dark abrasiveness of the larger society. Unlike the era's more epic-minded writers, Kromer and Cain portray every move of the dispossessed as a roundabout dance of futility. Where Cain's narrators remain elliptical even while setting up their murderous "accidents," Kromer's language becomes a dripping salve, running over and over the callous and hopeless everyday routines of millions during the Depression, including Kromer himself (his book was written in a CCC camp; debilitating illness brought on by several years as a hobo and rail rider eighty-sixed his later efforts). *Waiting for Nothing* becomes a sort of parody of the actual tedious "working grind" of the socialized man, whose way of life seems as remote and even humorous to Kromer as the eggs-n-yeggs milieu of the crime novels now seem to us. Kromer was not a crime writer except in the sense that he viewed society itself as criminal, but this militantly critical attitude is one shared consistently, if in more modulated tones, by the writers of American noir.

Several of the writers in the anthology were even more closely aligned, by either association or emulation, with the proletarian impulse, and the ways in which they are received and recalled today speaks to the gap between a "popular" (yet considered anti-intellectual in its time) genre and a "populist" (yet politically suspect) one. Kenneth Fearing was already a well-regarded poet known for undiluted leftist sentiment when he published his fourth novel, *The Big Clock*, in 1946. The novel's "ensemble" narration both reflects the smugness of the book's publishing-conglomerate setting and conceals Fearing's politicized "voice" to a degree his poetry rarely does. The quasi-criminal desire that informs the protagonists of all these novels is here manifested in Organization Man terms: the corporate honeycomb as voyeur's paradise, the addictive power of the perks, and what the yups of any era never understand—how easily one's participation in the money dance can become one's grinding end and devourer. Although the melodramatic plot—a crime magazine editor, framed for murder, is forced to hunt himself—may creak like an old Philco, the creeping horror of work inside a media conglomerate and the gassy authenticity of Fearing's callously relaxed protagonist remain effective. Fearing's commercial fortunes fell rapidly, however, especially after the FBI officially labeled him as a "potential" Communist in 1950, and having made little money from the film sale of his best known novel, he drifted into obscurity and a staff job at *Newsweek*.

Chester Himes, read today primarily as a seminal African-American writer, remains the Missing Man of classic crime fiction. Like Thompson's debut effort, Himes's first novel, *If He Hollers Let Him Go* (1946), is also set in the labor furnace of wartime California. Here a young black shipyard worker finds that the casual treachery of his white co-workers, the rigorous segregation of "public" life, and the harrying patriotism of the war effort essentially derive from the same shadowy system. As with Thompson and Hammett, Himes's hard-edged leftist perspective was forged from experience, rather than through the cooler routes of the academy. And, again like Thompson, Himes would evolve from the workerist style to a more individuated consideration of social authority. Himes's own break with the American left came early, when he offended his core audience with *Lonely Crusade* (1947), a chilly portrayal of a young black pawn in the midst of a UCLA "red conspiracy." Like Thompson and Fearing before him, Himes came to write crime novels accidentally, and in his case literally in exile: Living abroad in 1956, he was recruited by Marcel Duhamel, the editor of the French detective line Série Noire, to produce "police procedurals." The result was a series of eight "Harlem Domestic" novels featuring a memorably sorrowful/brutal duo of black detectives, Coffin Ed Jones and Grave Digger Johnson. These are intricately plotted urban picaresques, dense with Himes's recollection of both Harlem's sensual pleasures and the creeping rot beneath, a place where Jones and Johnson loom as enforcers of a weighted ghetto code. *The Real Cool Killers* (1959), Himes's representation in the Library of America anthology, is a comparatively slow and stationary fiction in which the apparent killer of a white soda pop salesman (who paid young black schoolgirls to take his fierce whippings) is snatched from the detectives by a "gage" smoking gang of faux-Arabic teenagers, the Real Cool Moslems. In tracking the gang down, Himes' detectives are more a roving version of Harlem's anarchy than representatives

of a comforting "downtown" social order. In its sharply etched portrayal of black-on-black cruelty and of the appetite of dispossessed youth for fantasy allegiances, the book is weirdly prescient. Like all these writers at their best, Himes used the knuckleheaded stylings of crime fiction to produce something more: a fully realized portrait of the black city's street life, social stratification, and underground economy, a document of a people beset by a rigged game and illicit temptations.

II.

As the small paperback houses reached their commercial apogee during the Fifties, the crime fiction they published became increasingly estranged from the left, even as the left itself turned away from its more inclusive proletarian past. It's telling that Mickey Spillane came to personify the genre in the public mind in those years: His seven original Mike Hammer novels, universally condemned for their "sado-fascist" tendencies while moving some fifteen million units, told of the widening chasm between the unwashed of the working class and their affronted intellectual betters.

Meanwhile, more marginal crime writers pursued increasingly interior and personalized fictions. Charles Willeford, author of at least seventeen crime novels, seems to flicker and fade as a human presence against his improbable early fiction. Willeford joined the Army Air Corps at sixteen, served as a tank commander in Europe in World War II, and remained in uniform for over a decade more while becoming a self-taught novelist, eventually publishing a string of kinky, truncated novels with some lower-rent paperback houses. These books are meticulous portrayals of the American alpha-male as social bayonet, welding a lush evocation of the swinging bachelor life ("We drank the shaker of stingers and went to bed") to the unsettling narrative perspective of all the sociopathic women-chasers whose scrim of tawdry macho recklessness is still celebrated today in the high tide of Cocktail Nation drivel. Willeford's second novel, *Pick Up* (1955), presents an odd variant on this approach: a meandering romance between a restless lunchroom attendant and an attractive woman whose tendency toward drunkenness dwarfs his. Although any description of the book makes it sounds like cheap romantic tragedy, Willeford's narrative is not maudlin or exploitative voyeurism. What strikes one are the inflections of delicacy and domestic concern which Willeford sneakily highlights, as in the minutiae of the protagonist's fruitless attempts to keep the couple in T-bones and whisky without holding a steady job. Unlike their prewar predecessors, Willeford's characters carry on a hungry romance with normality and all its accompanying sense of male entitlement. Like the lonesome sideburn-toting cocktail boys of our moment, clad in their spectral rayon, they wear the skins of conformists even as they explode in slow-mo in their greasy spoons, seedy bars, drunk wards, and jail cells.

III.

The appearance of Polito's ample anthology signals a canonical apogee of sorts for the fetishized revival of crime fiction that began in the early Eighties. That this revival has been often superficial is demonstrated by the disproportionate attention usually paid to the voluptuous, oil-painted cover art of the paperback originals: Reproduced in glossy postcard books and endlessly rehashed in film and advertising and rock band imagery, it is these unambiguous images that have resonated most powerfully for American consumers of the Eighties and Nineties. These static scenes are what we remember, what we intimately recall. But Polito's anthology presents different problems. Nearly all of its eleven novels function, on some level, as angry critiques of American-style capitalism, accusing it of degrading the average, nonprivileged citizen to the level of the criminal. And yet these novels' relationship to the proletarian writing of their time has almost never been considered. Nor are they likely to be read as social texts now.

No, these novels are remembered as legitimation, as a crude pedigree for the decontextualized-violence-product being excreted by the Culture Trust these days after its long process of profit-entertain-

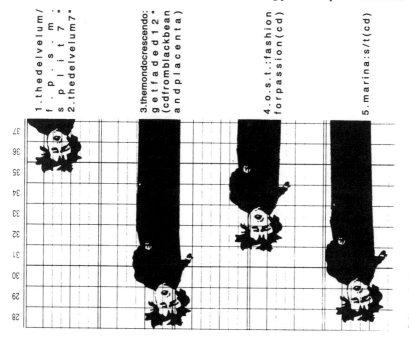

ment calculation and digestion. Just as the hipster embrace of the primitive pornography of nudie loops and girlie mags removes them from the racist and sexist Fifties "smoker" milieu, the chic elevation of noir occurs even while real-life criminal violence becomes ever more exclusively the province of an emerging polyethnic mystery class, about whom we generally hear only when individual incidents are horrific enough to merit close coverage. Both the pious, vampiric attentions of the news programs and the fetishized ghost of noir serve to obscure for consumers the ways in which the reconfiguring of violence is anything but accidental. In the cities, where the gentrification of decrepit areas has played its own role in the redistribution of crime, young urbanites (themselves steeped in noir accessorization) are now free to lounge in their "edgy" rehabbed apartments (exposed brick! Eurokitchens!) and luxuriate in the voyeuristic simulacrum of popcult perversion, zapped on the chemicals of their choice (Cosmopolitans, doobies, smack?), free from either police or criminal invasion, secure in the knowledge that by the bright light of day their employed lives will resume. In these same cities, mere blocks away, of course, the scales of safety and danger for different citizens are much jiggered. In the suburbs and in the "heartland," in the gated communities and on the New Jersey highways where the state smokeys still use race profiling in their traffic stops, the disconnect between public fear and public risk is even greater.

None of this detracts from the relief one feels that the Library of America anthology (and despite the smugness of its demographic, the Vintage crime line) ensures that these novels are again widely available, nor from the respect one must grant writers such as Fearing, Thompson, and Himes for surviving absurdities of circumstance that would turn most young writers today into publicists and salesmen, as well as for their audacity in insisting that

the thrill-driven potboiler (a genre fundamentally welded to the market) could still connect to real humanity despite the hackneyed plots of safes, yeggs, and fast black sedans. The quiet storms of these novels remain inviting against a contemporary aesthetic where the subtleties of real violence are lost in the universal translator, dumbed down into a single sick joke. What real murder or heist or cabal can reach us—can touch us with the fundamentally perverse and recognizable human impulses of the perpetrators—now that we all know enough to appreciate the zany humor of hitman John Travolta "accidentally" firing a .45 hollowpoint into the skinny guy's head, getting hitman Samuel Jackson's kool ride all fucked up with brains and shit? It's funny, we respond, in unison, as the synthetic blood patters down, as the Pepsi-drinking hitman rants on the big screen. We may flinch and giggle, but we're not particularly surprised or concerned, because what we're viewing bears no more familiarity or relevance to our lives than, say, a spectacle of giant gore-spraying gladiator insects. Despite their hoary vintage, the best of classic American crime writing offers no such divorce from prosaic reality, and it's this element that makes them still convincing and sometimes chilling, and that weaves into even a book as gray and personal as David Goodis's *Down There* (1956) an undeniably political consciousness. For readers who no longer recognize the fear that lurks behind everyday normality, these novels will seem only dated. But the curious circumstances these long buried writers portrayed are still with us—the too-quiet cafe, the too-helpful lawman, the darkness just beyond our brightly lit spaces—and as the news reports from such ordinary, frightened places as Junction City and Jonesboro confirm, we still live in a country where the civil dance of white flight—lock the door! dial 911!—is but a placebo in the face of ever more probable collisions, a lame imitation of the safety we crave.

—**Mike Newirth**

Rue des Blancs Manteaux

Certainly objects—places—writhe with uncertainty,
Not ours about them but their own. Promiscuous colors,
The summer truths. He was in love with yellow but unfaithful
With blue every chance he got. The sun kept the dayjail,
The nightjail had no keeper at all—his eyelids stuttered in both,
In both he wore his cell through the streets like a beautiful coat.
His friends published a list of his crimes in the paper ending
With Mythomania. The cops brought candy years later
To be remembered as a nature of things—a sweetness.

Return to Rue des Blancs Manteaux

When we arrived it was much as we expected, we had
Sent out imaginings ahead to do the dirty work: a small arch
On a street of windows gang'd with ghostly wedding gowns
Opening onto a sudden place which wanted us—all this
In the late afternoon beneath the balcony of having to return.

—Joshua Clover

Cordon Sanitaire

MIKE O'FLAHERTY

Rockerdämmerung

While "late" capitalism has failed to deal the long-promised death-blows to "ideology" and "history," it did manage a trick that likely took even Francis Fukuyama by surprise: It has killed rock 'n' roll. There was an eerie parallel between the fate of rock's avant-garde and that of the former Soviet Union in the Nineties. The moment of truth came in 1991, when the Soviet Union dissolved itself and loud rock band Nirvana's major-label debut, *Nevermind*, hit No. 1 on the charts. The "indie rock" scene and the Soviet Union had both defined themselves by their opposition to monopoly capital.[†] Now their vast and hitherto untapped resources were available for exploitation—or, in the more reciprocal language favored by both IMF officials and recording industry A&R men, "development." In both cases the corporate overlords were full of hope that their new friends would provide the growth necessary to stave off crisis and stagnation. But in both cases the lucrative new properties were squandered and laid to waste.

At the dawn of the Nineties the Big Six[‡] corporations that dominate the recording industry faced the prospect of a protracted sales slump on the order of the 1979-82 postdisco debacle. The industry had managed to recover from that slump by cramming the Top 40 with appropriated black and British styles, but by the end of the Eighties these, too, were bland and codified, and yielded diminishing returns. The handful of media-saturated superstars who had so recently served as public symbols of industry's recovery were (with the exception of Madonna) proving unable to retain audiences as stable and profitable as those of their "classic rock" predecessors. The fate of the recovery's third element, heavy metal, was more complicated. During the Eighties, the metal audience had bifurcated into rock ("thrash") and pop ("glam") factions. Thrash's purist extremism of form and content deliberately limited its sales reach. But that purist extremism also did terrible damage to glam's street cred: It made glam look "fake" by comparison. Something more commercially palatable than thrash would have to be found to take advantage of glam's yawning authenticity gap.

Punk rock did not seem a likely candidate to save the recording industry in the Nineties. In fact, punk's complete commercial failure, along with that of nearly all the early "postpunk" and "new wave" acts, played a considerable role in precipitating the 1979-82 industry bust. Like thrash metal, punk functioned entirely as a negative genre, returning nothing financially but inflicting fatal credibility wounds on such proven bottom-line performers as disco

---

† The term "indie rock" will here denote music derived from punk rock (though often by a few degrees of separation); released on a record label not owned outright by the Big Six record companies (corporate distribution is an even more controversial issue); and rooted to some extent in rock forms while investing them with an eccentricity and/or abrasiveness alien to the mainstream, major-label rock of the given moment.

‡ The Big Six, at the time, were Warner-Electra-Atlantic (WEA), Sony (formerly CBS), BMG (formerly RCA), Polygram, Universal (formerly MCA), and Thorn-EMI. Polygram and BMG merged in 1998, incidentally generating massive layoffs—then there were five.

and album-oriented rock (or "AOR," the once-vanguard format that ossified almost instantly into "classic rock"). But while thrash had carved out a small but profitable subculture niche within the labyrinth of the Big Six, punk and its immediate successors went nowhere commercially. True, a group of vaguely postpunk acts tailored for major-label success ("new wave") had once generated some income for the Big Six, but each succeeding wave of signings from the postpunk underground met the same disastrous commercial fate as the punk founders, usually losing their original audience to boot.

Then, in the guise of Nirvana and a few "Alternative"[†] satellites, punk rock finally paid its debt to society. It made its peace with the market. The original punks (and their truest successors) had declared war on all other music subcultures, and those audiences had responded in kind. Alternative promised precisely the reverse: The new sound seemed to offer something for everybody. To hard rock devotees, it combined the street cred, heaviness, and speed of thrash with glam's pop sense and Seventies trad-rock familiarity: In other words, it promised a return to what metal had been before the great glam/thrash schism. To new-wave trendy types—the people who were "alternative" before alternative was Alternative—it offered the frisson of apparent avant-gardism and a new and insurgent wardrobe to match. To hippies of all ages still high on the myth of rock as youth movement, it offered the prospect of an anti-establishment white youth music with genuine mass appeal for perhaps the first time since Altamont. And to the Big Six, it offered more than just a

way out of a slump: This was nothing less than the new paradigm, a *renewal*. A new constellation of stars was called for, both big and small, along with fresh styles of publicity and a cornucopia of lifestyle tie-ins. Along with hip-hop, which was finally breaking commercially around this time, and the CD's replacement of vinyl, Alternative solved several problems at once.

Independent American punk rock had begun the Eighties dedicated to the destruction of the corporate music industry and the political and aesthetic values it stood for. Ten years later, now calling itself "Alternative," it was playing a crucial role in saving the Big Six from economic collapse. What happened?

From its very inception, British punk rock had aimed to free itself from the production and distribution networks of the Big Six. The early British independent labels—such as Raw, Beggars Banquet, Step Forward, and dozens of others too tiny and ephemeral to be remembered—formed as a matter of grass-roots pragmatism, essentially to accommodate the punks' fleeting and careless enthusiasms; you didn't have to wait to be "discovered." Oddly enough, most of these labels fell victim to punk's very success. The genre's supernova—the salad days of 1977 when it seemed that punk was going to destroy or absorb the Big Six on its own terms—appeared to vitiate the need to maintain and nurture independent labels for their own sake.

The Sex Pistols' spectacular auto-destruction,[‡] however, gave independence a new significance and a new political charge. A crucial portion of the British punk movement concluded that the celebrity framework into which the Pistols had been fitted trivialized their politics

---

[†] "Alternative" as a musical genre has been most narrowly defined as a slick commercial version of the late-Eighties "Seattle sound" associated with indie label Sub Pop—a sound that grafted dissonant, plodding postpunk guitar grind onto song structures derived from early-Seventies hard rock. Though this was indeed the dominant strain, Alternative was actually comprised of various slick commercial versions of nearly the full gamut of late-Eighties indie rock. One might even say that alternative combined the sound of Eighties indie rock with the sensibility of Eighties "new wave" or "new music"—the MTV- and radio-oriented guitar-based pop-rock which was the first rock music officially designated "alternative" by the music industry. (Not for nothing did embittered hair-metal loyalist Chuck Eddy compare Nirvana to forgotten Eighties jangle-guitar popsters Let's Active and the Del Fuegos.)

[‡] Disgusted by manager Malcolm McLaren's increasing resort to cheap publicity stunts, as well as his attempts to screw the band members financially, vocalist Johnny Rotten abruptly quit the Pistols in January 1978, immediately after the last show of their chaotic American tour. (His parting remark to the audience: "Ever had the feeling you've been cheated?") In one fell swoop Rotten deprived the record industry of the leading icons on which the marketing of punk would have depended.

of confrontation into a circus of self-destructive outrage. These "postpunks" now regarded indie labels as permanent counter-institutions in explicit opposition to the Big Six. Though American record collectors may not know it, the postpunk labels (particularly the greatest of them, London's Rough Trade) were thus part of the tide of political radicalism that swept Britain in 1978-79 and that culminated in a massive strike wave that shut the country down. Rough Trade people were active in the SWP, a powerful Trotskyist caucus in the Labor Party. Political radicalism was built into the postpunk model, and its implications would reverberate through American indie in the political big sleep of the Reagan years like a half-remembered promise.

In the Eighties, American indie labels more or less followed in the footsteps of their British peers. American punk bands courted by fashion-conscious A&R men in 1977 were abruptly abandoned the following year, and no further offers were forthcoming. As had early British punk, the first wave of American punk went the indie route simply because nobody else was willing to release their work. Before long, though, the most prominent and emblematic American indie labels (Homestead and SST, among others) embraced the postpunk model of secession and opposition to the majors.

Southern California was far and away America's most prolific and inventive punk scene during the crucial few years following 1978. In

response to what seemed a permanent quarantine by the Big Six, Southern Californians developed American punk's first durable institutions and elaborated the affectingly quixotic worldview punk would bequeath to indie rock: a tenacious adherence to unrealizable utopian aspirations, and a principled commitment to "action," no matter how ineffectual or absurd. The early L.A. scene took comfort, even reveled, in its own absurdity. It had to; while poverty and political upheaval were palpable to their British counterparts, American punks repined in sunny, suffocating prosperity and near-universal political apathy. There, at the heart of the American empire, the mass-cultural contradictions of Seventies America reached a point of hysterical exaggeration: A cult of "niceness" and bland self-indulgence strained to hold back the numbing fear that the economic and military walls protecting the prosperity and security of the great American middle were crumbling. The early L.A. punks cheered on the collapse, hoping for a new world of danger and surprise, of extreme sensations and emotions. They didn't make many friends around town.

L.A. punk turned social isolation itself into a virtue. The thrill of secrecy, something utterly alien to the British style, was a recurring theme (consider X's "The Unheard Music" and the Germs' "What We Do Is Secret"). This, too, became a crucial element of what American indie was all about. In the rosy-fingered dawn of hip capitalism, anything you could think of was now a marketable commodity, and overexposure domesticated even the most shocking features of contemporary life: the neutron bomb, Three Mile Island, brutal pornography, and the Sex Pistols. If you wanted to find L.A. punk (and indie rock after it), you had to discover it. Secrecy restored mystery and adventure to a numbingly familiar world: What looked like an abandoned porn theater was actu-

JAY RYAN

ally the venue where the police- and club-banned Germs were playing tonight under a pseudonym.

But secrecy did not mean secession. The punks were looking out at the world from their hiding places, and the L.A. punk world was itself a kind of looking-glass version of the "real" world: Familiar social and cultural styles were grotesquely mimicked and put to perverse and idiosyncratic uses. The "serious" social and political issues that mattered to "informed" people were defiantly summarized as dirty jokes. The greatest inversion of all—and the one which survived longest as punk turned to indie and gradually accommodated itself to the outside world—was to find such inventive and audacious work being done in a format as seemingly banal and familiar as rock. It was this feeling of having stumbled into looking-glass land that gave the discovery of punk (and later indie, when it was good) its thrill, whether one found out about it through a friend, a record store, an all-ages show, a fanzine, a radio station, whatever. That discovery was like the moment in the film *They Live* when Rowdy Roddy Piper puts on a pair of shoddy-looking sunglasses and sees that the Reagan-era yuppies around him are actually space aliens who have enslaved the world. Punk showed you what the "real" world really looked like.

This impact was made possible by a restless formal adventurousness which in three years took L.A. punk far beyond its initial British models. The most daring of the Hollywood punks and the suburban kids who soon followed them gradually developed a formal language that broke with rock tradition far more radically than had the British punks, who were rooted in the Sixties' British Invasion sound. L.A.'s new formal language came to be called "hardcore." Above all it meant playing fast, but the new demands posed by speed forced the musicians to take previously unthinkable liberties with song structure. Melody and comprehensible lyrics were discarded when they got in the way. Songs sped up and slowed down suddenly, ended in the middle of a verse,

inverted their chord progressions halfway through. Where previously most punk (to say nothing of the rest of rock) had tried to express original ideas through an inherited, unexamined formal language, now those forms could be adjusted to fit the ideas. If you had a ten-second idea, you could write a ten-second song.

The suburban L.A. hardcore kids surpassed their Hollywood godfathers and -mothers by making punk accessible for the first time to people outside of a "hip," style-conscious milieu. (The Minutemen, hardcore pioneers from the working-class L.A. suburb of San Pedro, later admitted to an interviewer how "uncool" they felt when they first made the Hollywood scene.) Hardcore expressed a newly comfortable and honest sense of place and identity, no matter how "uncool" such subjects were. This enabled the music to rapidly break out of the bohemian ghetto, where most American punk had previously been confined, and travel to D.C., Boston and the Midwest. The first full-fledged L.A. hardcore records appeared in 1980; a mere two years later dozens of bands, such as D.C.'s Void, Michigan's Negative Approach, and Boston's SS Decontrol, were releasing records that surpassed most of the L.A. originators in stylistic daring and sonic extremism. Hardcore gave a potentially huge group of suburban kids a language to engage directly with their specific social context, rather than some faux-universal music-industry fantasy that had nothing to do with anybody's ordinary life. It also generated a vibrant regionalism which would sustain indie rock as well. Still, hardcore remained totally shut out by the Big Six. But the genre's exclusion created a space for both local scenes and the American punk independent labels, such as L.A.'s SST, Michigan's Touch and Go, and D.C.'s Dischord. And hardcore framed its mutual hostility with the Big Six in the context of its larger hostility to the emerging social world of Reaganite America, a world the hardcore kids knew with the intimacy of a personal grudge: Transnational corporations sold narcotizing pop music to their mall-mad peers and transferred the profits to their missile-development subsidiaries.

Hardcore's radicalism soon began to sound as prefabricated as corporate rock itself. Instead of attacking the actual militarists or consumerists around them, bands began to attack an abstract "militarism" or "consumerism." This development stemmed from the emergence of a handful of hardcore institutions large and powerful enough to wield disproportionate influence over once-autonomous local scenes. Abandoning the humor and realism that had leavened hardcore's insurrectionary pretensions, these institutions reduced hardcore's politics and aesthetics to rote in the name of movement "unity." Most notable was the San Francisco-based fanzine *Maximum RockNRoll*. The band Culturcide best summed up *MRR*'s astonishing reach and homogenizing force: "I've been all around this great big world and there's punks wherever you go/ But they all wanna see their scene report in Maximum RockNRoll/ They wish they all could be California punks. . . ." This predictability, along with hardcore's fanatical formal purism, contributed to its

rapid petrifaction into formula. But hardcore's free-ranging hostility and ruthless self-consciousness also inspired its smartest adherents to go still further in challenging the audience and themselves. Think of Minor Threat's obsessive jihad against that most intimate and hallowed of rock rituals, getting fucked-up before the show; or Flipper (and later Black Flag) playing as slow as they could for audiences who'd come to expect high-speed background noise suitable for the mosh pit. Indie rock had arrived.

Unlike hardcore, "indie rock" did not have a single distinctive sound; in fact, it emerged largely as a reaction to hardcore's increasing stylistic rigidity. The common thread uniting the archetypal LPs Minutemen, Hüsker Dü, the Replacements made in indie's watershed year, 1984, is an almost manic eclecticism, ranging from eerie drumless interludes to ragged noise-gush, set in conscious defiance of *MRR*-style demands for a straitjacket beat for unified-punk-youth to march or mosh to for The Cause. Yet however disparate the styles explored on these records, each album remained of a piece: an integrated, thought-out aesthetic and worldview lay behind them, and their greater complexity (especially in comparison to contemporary hardcore) necessitated a commensurately complex stylistic range. Indie's aesthetic ideals—musical originality and expression of a personal but compelling worldview—were so banal that scenesters were often embarrassed to state them explicitly, but for once the music itself more than vindicated them.

At the same time, though, the move from hardcore to indie saw the first glimmerings of aesthetic deradicalization that would later explode with Alternative. Reasoning that bad music reflected a dysfunctional society and culture, punk and hardcore bands had built impressive solidarity around an explicit rejection of commercial rock and its trappings—especially rock's Sixties-era mystique of individual genius. Indie rock smuggled a sort of star system back into the underground. Where the leading indie labels, such as SST and Homestead, once had documented the constantly shifting cast of characters of a local scene, they now focused, naturally enough, on the long-term development of a handful of outstanding artists with no relationship other than their label affiliation. Where egalitarian punk and hardcore movement cultures had forced artists to confront the social context and implications of their work in a constant conversation with other people, the new heroes of indie rock could simply plead that Fifth Amendment of bohemianism, "self-expression." And where hardcore had constituted itself as a self-contained counterworld—the Big Six's absolute negative mirror-image—indie's rock fusionists discovered that they could create music that resembled familiar rock styles but was "better" (an impression reinforced by rave reviews from mainstream rock critics who had ignored or despised punk and hardcore). The Big Six noticed the shift, and by 1984 they began to express interest.

Two of the best and most prominent early indie bands, Minneapolis's Hüsker Dü and the Replacements, made major-label deals in 1985, and the indie scene observed their unfolding fate with no small interest. Hüsker Dü's music was becoming gradually more timid and circumspect even before they were signed by Warner Bros. The band's lyrics moved away from engagement with the social world and toward more "personal" concerns; in mainstream rock culture this move is traditionally associated with increased "maturity," and so it was hailed by the mainstream rock press. At the same time, though, the band's increasing lyrical introversion was accompanied by growing formal complacency and diminished passion in performance. The Replacements' stylistic shift was even more dramatic, so much so that many fans suspected they'd been coerced by Sire into changing their sound: By their second major-label release the once chaotic band was playing "tight," Stonesy bar-band rock. The band itself seemed deeply confused about what it wanted. The video for their first Sire single, "Bastards of Young," consisted entirely of a static shot of a record player; but this visual middle finger to the Big Six (and MTV) was cover for what seemed a blatant attempt on singer Paul Westerberg's part to write a catchy youth anthem.

Both Hüsker Dü and the Replacements retained an instinctive fury and eccentricity that resisted any attempts to make their sound commercially palatable; in retrospect their slow unraveling has a poignant quality. At the time, however, a humiliated indie-rock audience responded by vehemently rejecting everything those bands were imagined to stand for. The use of traditional rock forms quickly became deeply suspect, and the genre's leadership passed to a handful of more experimental bands like Sonic Youth, Big Black, and the Butthole Surfers. At the most basic level, audiences turned against nothing less than the Minneapolis bands' heart-on-my-sleeve sincerity, which now seemed more than ever to dovetail with familiar classic rock banalities (think Bob Seger). Savvier musicians abandoned emotion for sensation—the purer and more wrenching the better—and the confessional for an ambiguity that left tantalizingly open the degree of the artist's identification with his or her (often un-savory) subject.

In many ways this change improved indie rock immeasurably. The new music restored an element of confrontation with the audience. The musicians seemed to have a homing instinct for the most brutally physical aspects of every previous punk and postpunk genre; they fused them into a sound of unprecedented force and visceral pleasure. In terms of sheer stylistic sophistication and formal command, punk and indie reached their pinnacle during the second half of the Eighties. But there were problems as well, complications that would eventually prove fatal. The best bands seemed to be those who were most obsessive and extreme in developing some aspect of indie rock's formal language to its logical end point. (One of my personal favorites, the D.C./N.Y.C. band Pussy Galore, released a series of records between 1985 and 1988 which, in a progressively refined and deadly manner, imagined what the British Invasion and U.S. garage rock bands would have sounded like if their music had actually been the socially toxic hate-noise its contemporary critics absurdly considered it to be. Listening to this band's astonishing, beautiful work, it seemed that they were probing the limits of a potential for cathartic violence and sensuality within those forms, a potential whose very existence had barely even dawned on others. Yet these qualities made Pussy Galore's music feel strangely suffocating as well; it was as if they were driven to reach a point where no further development of rock would be possible, for them or anybody else.)

The indie scene's disengagement from the social world continued, even accelerated; increasingly, the main subject and interest of indie rock was indie rock. Even politics soon seemed just another variety of the hated "sincerity." About the only credible attitude left for the knowing yet aspiring rocker, it seemed, was irony: embracing illicit social identities, banal musical styles, and so forth, then leaving it up to the audi-ence to decide how seriously to take it (if at all). It was a delicate balancing act, and some did fall, undone by their own posturing. Perhaps the most dramatic such instance was the fate of the Dwarves, a band that fastidiously cultivated a reputation for violence in both their music and behavior. In 1992 the band announced to the world that its guitarist had been stabbed to death. It soon emerged that he had merely left the group; the remaining Dwarves apparently had decided to use his departure to enhance their menacing legend. Enraged, Sub Pop dropped them in the very year the label's famous alums Nirvana were completing their conquest of mainstream rock. The two events form an eerily appropriate capstone to the indie-rock era.

Indie rock's ironic style was useful, initially, as a kind of game of intellectual "chicken": The threat of being informed that the latest hip thing they'd fervently embraced was actually a joke at their expense might (in theory) lead people to think harder about what they really liked and why. Problem was, in its increasing insularity and disengagement, the indie scene was less inclined to use irony as a critical weapon than to make it a snotty parlor trick. As it was, indie-rock irony rapidly took the path of least resistance: You could

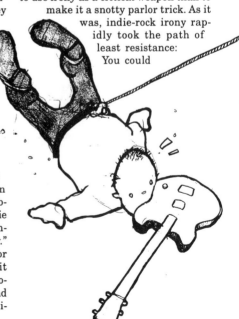

sidestep composer's block—or the absence of talent, as the case may be—by retreating to banal forms comfortably familiar to you and your audience and claiming that it was actually a wry comment on rock's formal impasse. Punk and hardcore had used sarcasm, but almost naively, as a way of expressing strongly held opinions. Indie-rock irony, by contrast, belied a fear above all of embarrassment, of being passionate or holding any convictions—of not being cool.

Perhaps the saddest example of this phenomenon was the career of Urge Overkill. On their earlier records, such as 1989's *Jesus Urge Superstar*, Urge deployed the mildewed, time-ridiculed sounds of Seventies "classic" rock to conjure up a world of the forlorn and forgotten and vanished, a world where pleasure and beauty were no less real for being restricted to dusty, bittersweet memories—a world, most importantly, bigger and more affecting than any rock genre in and of itself. Slowly but surely, however, Urge shifted from using Seventies rock trappings (and archaic showbiz trappings) to express a deeply idiosyncratic and poignant worldview to embodying those trappings because they afforded cheap, lazy "fun" to performers and audience alike. It was a horrible thing to witness, like watching a suit absorb its wearer. There was still the occasional great song, but the band mainly protected its credibility by emphasizing the overblown, ridiculous aspects of their persona: like, if these guys have so much distance from their work, they must be really smart and there must be some important point to the "joke." But the prospect of actual rock-stardom eroded the protective irony that had precariously elevated Urge over the cesspool of their cheesy source material: In 1993, Urge released a major-label debut which, but for its glossy Nineties production and a few witty lyrics, was utterly indistinguishable from the most banal Seventies hard rock. The band had outsmarted itself: It seemed too palpably fake and corny to fully click with the authenticity-obsessed alternakids.

Urge's second major-label album tanked, and their career soon sputtered to an overdue finish.

By the late Eighties, the indie scene was largely composed of people who had grown up in the Seventies or of their little brothers and sisters. This was the demographic basis for indie rock's most significant and influential ironic rediscovery: Seventies-style hard rock and metal. Seattle pioneers Green River's great *Come On Down* EP of 1985 heralded this sound (although punk of the Flipper/Black Flag variety was perhaps more evident). Only with the 1987 debut EP of Seattle's Soundgarden (one of the first Sub Pop records) did a band with vocal and rhythmic approaches derived from Seventies hard rock make a strong impact on the indie scene. Within a year Sub Pop, the Seattle label most closely associated with Seventies hard rock revivalism, was a household word in indieland. And Seventies-oriented indie bands were now appearing by the dozens, not only in Seattle but across the country. It was a return to the womb, with all the comfortable insularity and effortless self-gratification that implied.

This is not to deny the greatness of the best Seventies hard rock acts, or indeed their influence on punk itself; rather, it is merely to say that nearly all their indie-rock epigones now embraced their music out of intellectual and aesthetic cowardice and failure of nerve, adding little to the source material and living parasitically on it like suckfish attached to the belly of a sodden, dying whale. White Zombie, unlike most, initially did something genuinely novel and adventurous with their Seventies source material. But by their second album, even they were playing that material far more "straight"; a twelve-inch Kiss cover came next, followed by a major-label deal. To disappointed fan Lydia Lunch, "it sounded like they had some blood sucked." Some denounced this *nostalgie de la boue*,[†] but indie rock had long since abandoned the critical basis for a counter-attack. In a scene that fetishized the artist's pursuit of his or her whims,

---

[†] Gerard Cosloy speculating in 1990 on Soundgarden's indie-scene popularity: "Is it because most of you idiots secretly long to go back to junior high when you smoked pot all day and actually understood the simple music you listened to?"

Me-Decade retreads could even constitute a fuck-you to the conformity imposed by the punk-rock thought police ("You want us to go back to playing fuckin' hardcore?"). And if that still didn't convince you, well, you "just didn't get it," were "taking it too seriously," etc.

Irony ultimately made the crucial difference in indie rock's long-awaited commercial breakthrough as Alternative. Audiences had already been acclimated, of course, to traditional rock styles, and they appreciated the punk and indie seasoning the new bands provided to make them seem so fresh. But more than that: Irony killed the scene's obsessive suspicion of betrayal that had been so evident during the Hüsker/Replacements debacle, and substituted in its place a confident sense that the artist was eternally distanced from his or her actions, or their consequences. In the most generic descriptive terms, these bands were making commercially accessible rock music for the Big Six. But the ironic sensibility could explain this as a mocking commentary on same— or (if you were really smart) a bold critique of the hypocrisy of those who claimed to be above such things.

Urge's experience—the sudden raising of commercial hopes to levels unthinkable in the indie Eighties, followed by the rapid obliteration of those hopes along with the bands themselves—epitomized the trajectory of alternative in the first half of the Nineties. Nirvana's major-label debut *Nevermind*, released in the fall of 1991 to little media fanfare, had topped the *Billboard* charts by Christmas. Though in retrospect one can see how indie rock's development through the Eighties prepared the ground for the alternative breakthrough, at the time that breakthrough seemed somehow flukish or miraculous. America's cultural punditocracy was baffled. It was quickly agreed that this had something to do with "disaffected youth" (one had seen this sort of thing before), that these kids resented their hippie/yuppie parents, that they adored flannel and opiates. But as the media catalog of alleged alternative paraphernalia expanded, it became less and less clear what (if anything) it added up to—one could make a case that virtually anything was part of such an amorphous entity.

Certainly the Big Six felt itself on unfamiliar ground; rather than be caught napping by the next unpredictable development of this new popular taste, it was better to be on the safe side and sign everybody. By 1993, acts whose terminal idiosyncrasy and blatant listener-unfriendliness had long been running jokes even within the indie scene now found themselves uneasily ensconced in some Big Six sinecure. (I remember well my shock and amusement in the summer of 1994 to discover, at Tower Records in New York City, that Daniel Johnston—an artist then best known for violently erratic public behavior, frequent hospitalization for mental "issues," fervent claims of divine inspiration, and wonderful home recordings which tended to evoke a PCP-addled ten-year-old warbling into a hand-held tape recorder over his dad's polka records—now dwelt in the hallowed stables of Atlantic Records, an organization known for such pillars of music-industry tradition as Otis Redding, Iron Butterfly and Bobby Darin.)

By 1994 Alternative had swept a large portion of the indie scene up into its temporarily triumphant crusade for total dominance of the youth market. Optimists construed the triumph of Alternative as a triumph for the punk rock ethos which had given birth to indie and, through it, to alternative; as if the seed of the Sex Pistols, kept alive through the years by indie rock, was now flowering under the sun of mass success Big Six-style. In reality Alternative finally effected a complete inversion of punk-rock values. Stylistic adventurousness faded as each Alternative success magnetically drew other bands to tailor their sound to the proven formula. Regional distinc-

tions dissolved as bands competed in a homogeneous national market and local scenes were signed up en masse before they'd even had a chance to develop a coherent collective identity. And Alternative's lack of engagement with the outside world was so complete that the very distinction between private angst and social criticism was blurred. On those rare occasions when Alternative figures addressed concrete social or political issues, their pronouncements were indistinguishable from the smug liberal platitudes traditionally associated with the aging Sixties mafia who still set the cultural tone of the record industry.

Indie rock still exists, sort of. A large minority within the indie scene was not able or willing to get signed; unfortunately, it almost seems as if they decided to fend off co-optation by making their music as repellently self-indulgent as possible. Indie rock's drift toward asocial introversion and the fetishization of the artist's whim have reached their grotesque apotheosis.[†] But the acute and inventive formal sense which once redeemed those tendencies has vanished. These groups aren't interested in crafting sharply defined musical forms that jump out and demand the listener's attention; maybe they view structure itself to be repressively "rockist," ironic in light of the fact that they've regressed to "jamming" aimlessly like stereotypical hippies. Indie rock still draws on other musics, but it now does so with the listless dilettantism of a yuppie Sunday-browsing through the ethnic-foods section at Treasure Island (cf. The Jon Spencer Blues Explosion). Indie artists seem driven only by the desire to be something, anything other than what

---

[†] And this is true not merely of the willfully obscure but even of many of the most prominent indie bands. Cat Power's music seems to exist in a hermetically sealed world. The music trickles along so anemically that one does not so much engage with it as observe it from a distance. Vocalist Chan Marshall sings like she's peeking at you from behind a curtain; if you make eye contact she will dart back into the darkness. The effect is to short-circuit the very possibility of communication between performer and listener. Jandek and (pre-boogie) Royal Trux often sounded something like this, but they spiked their lulling introversion with sudden bursts of disquieting sound and imagery; Cat Power's music rarely escapes its numb monotony. Still, Marshall's vocal and guitar work is often quite beautiful, enticing one with the possibility of something behind the mystery. Sadly, the same cannot be said of Tortoise. These undeniably inventive musicians do not shape their creations into striking, compelling forms. The group cultivates an open-ended quality, investing rock-derived music with a sense of entropy, as if it were spontaneously generated, like the sounds of everyday life. But in removing themselves from their work (or rather, concealing their presence), they seem not to realize that even the random sounds of everyday life will include by the very virtue of their indiscriminate quality some personality, some dynamic and emotional range—and perhaps most importantly, some real-world content.

they are. Punk and its truest indie descendants wanted to destroy and replace the rest of rock music because it was part of a world against which they had declared war. Indie rock now seems driven by a quest to find a safe hiding place away from rock music and the outside world itself. But if it's not rock, it's not anything else either; indeed, it barely exists. It lacks the sense of purpose and confidence to become something new and real.

Still, you can hardly blame indie for wanting to have nothing to do with rock music. What punk failed to do despite years of conscious effort—destroying mainstream rock music—Alternative did inadvertently. Post-hippie rock acts had kept their audiences stable and happy by keeping their expectations low. They promised to provide the hedonistic familiarity of Zep/Stones-derived rock music, and that's what they delivered. Alternative promised a full-blown cultural revolution, and it delivered . . . the hedonistic familiarity of Zep/Stones-derived rock music. Thus was created by 1996 a "credibility gap" of rock-historical magnitude. Having abandoned indie rock's formal ingenuity, the already stultifyingly formulaic Alternative scene degenerated rapidly into pathetic self-parody. Lionized in the media as the voice of a new generation, alternative believed its own hype, abandoning the wit and realism of punks whose genuine engagement with the world around them made them self-conscious of the absurd aspects of their project. By the time the solipsism and deliberate vagueness of its putative youth radicalism became impossible to hide, alternative's political pretensions had been so inflated that it proved impossible to retract them with any grace. This only added to the utter public humiliation its various artists suffered on the way to oblivion.

Alternative's sales curve was plunging by 1996, and it has not recovered. Nor has any other rock subgenre taken its place commercially. And for the first time in rock history, long-term recovery seems uncertain: The mass white youth market which sustained the various rock subgenres for a quarter century has largely abandoned rock altogether for hip-hop or r&b. Once-successful alternative bands attempt to revive their fortunes by employing potentially lucrative non-rock strategies: Marilyn Manson's new one was promoted as a move toward "electronica," while Hole attempted to get over via Courtney Love's prominence in a "synergistic" media world where celebrity shapes the perception of artistic merit and significance rather than vice versa. And despite this, and an avalanche of advance hype, the new albums of both groups flopped: The blatant attempt to distance them from the now-unhip rock scene may have made their rock content even more conspicuous. What remains of indie rock itself attempts such maneuvers: Labels that epitomized hip during the Alternative era now play a desperate game of catch-up, dabbling in "electronica," and the former supreme taste makers who run them now follow the lead of younger cognoscenti "native" to the new subgenres.

Despite it all, a handful of indie-rock acts persist in creating exciting music. They have survived because they remain attached to independent American punk rock's founding values while doing something new with them. The bands grouped around the Olympia, Washington indie label Kill Rock Stars, for example, embody everything that's still good about indie rock. The KRS bands could easily have signed on with the Big Six during the "riot grrl" moment a few years ago, yet not one of them has ever defected to the majors: The bands see themselves as part of a specific, ongoing radical political subculture (feminism filtered through punk autonomism) and regional music scene, of which the KRS label is an integral part. The music of bands like the Bangs and the Cold Cold Hearts inventively fuses disparate forms into a coherent and original whole: the regional heritage (primarily the distinctively heavy garage sound stretching from the Sonics to the U-Men), as well as the fragmented history of women in punk which the KRS scene has done much to reveal and articulate. Crucial to the KRS project is its love/hate relationship with hardcore. Motivated by hostility toward male domination of the hardcore (and indie) scene, KRS has consciously done for the young women of suburban America what hardcore did for their male counterparts: created a voice and formal language rooted in a specific social context. Like the best of its punk and indie predecessors, it's a new sound shaped to express a new kind of critical engagement with the world, from the immediate to the global.

Other bands are doing original and exciting work in the various subgenres nurtured by American independent labels—hardcore, garage rock, postpunk. This may not seem as exciting as what punk and indie rock seemed to promise between the Pistols and Nirvana: A permanent cultural revolution in which the music would continuously transform itself completely before it "got old." But with hindsight we can now see that this promise was illusory. Contempt for the past gradually stripped indie rock of the punk-derived core values which made it worth caring about in the first place. And it was no accident that what replaced them—Alternative—was so compatible with the values of the entertainment industry. Planned obsolescence, the promise of the new and improved, the sneer of willful cultural amnesia—these are the values of the marketplace, radical only in their destructiveness.

If indie rock has a future, it lies in the cultivation of a sense of its own past. When the Kill Rock Stars scene started, there were perhaps fewer women involved in punk or indie rock than ever before, but punk's ancient history offered the examples of Poly Styrene, Penelope Houston and others, and the KRS bands built on what they'd begun. The problem they faced is one which confronts all radicals today: The dead vacancy of the present culture, which consigns the past to the "dustbin of history," the better to lay infinite claim to the future. All around the world, people are losing their ability to imagine anything outside the eternal present of a

transnational corporate capitalism the depth and breadth of which now seems virtually limitless. And they are beginning to forget that anyone ever imagined something beyond it.

Twenty years ago the punks demanded far more than we even dare to imagine now, and behind them lay over a century of politics and art built on the idea that people can think and build far beyond the limits of the present. That expansive social imagination may be moribund now; we laugh at the conceit that a mass-market rock subculture can become the functional equivalent of a social or political movement. If a few million people care mildly about an art that advocates some conveniently vague "rebelliousness," it means nothing; their lives are barely touched by it. But if a few thousand people care deeply about an art which challenges them to question everything about the world around them and shows them that they have the power to make something different and better out of it, they may be inspired to transport that imaginative power from art to a project of real political and social change. At the very least they will see and feel more of the world they live in; the depth and creativity of their engagement with it will be immeasurably and irrevocably enhanced. And that's also a beginning.

The Hidden Injuries of Balance

SANDY ZIPP

The committee here from the Clothing Manufacturers Association are not in a position to give evidence concerning the so-called "sweating system." We are manufacturers. We give our work out by contract. If any pernicious system exists we do not know anything about it.

—Lewis Hornthal, president of the CMA, before Congress, 1892

BY some grim stroke of luck, the sweatshop reemerged as a *cause célèbre* a few years ago when California labor officials raided the now-notorious El Monte garment factory on the outskirts of Los Angeles. In this virtual prison, dozens of Thai immigrants, mostly women, toiled in conditions little better than slavery, sewing sportswear day and night for such concerns as Montgomery Ward, Mervyn's, B.U.M., and High Sierra. Shortly thereafter, thanks largely to a skillful campaign by union activists to publicize contemporary sweatshop outrages, Americans were treated to the rather surreal spectacle of cherished celebrities stunned by a temporary disordering of the consumerist chain of being. As Michael Jordan shrugged at the lot of Nike's subcontracted workers in Indonesia, as cloying rag impresario Kathie Lee Gifford tearfully remonstrated that she *just didn't know*, the sweatshop seemed destined, if not to spur a national examination of conscience, then at least to provide good tabloid TV.

Joining the media cavalcade a little late, the Smithsonian Institution's National Museum of American History tiptoed off the reservation of polite consensus history last year and staged *Between a Rock and a Hard Place: A History of American Sweatshops, 1820–Present*. (The show ended its run in D.C. this past December, and is tentatively scheduled to alight in Los Angeles at the Museum of Tolerance in September of this year.) In defiance of industry trade groups and congressional blowhards, the official center of American historical consciousness at first seemed determined to lift the shroud from the history of this international scourge. In the end, however, those who hoped the show might resurrect the spirit of the Popular Front Thirties—not to mention those who anticipated more cannon fodder for the culture wars—have reason to feel a little cheated. *Between a Rock and a Hard Place* turns out to be a underwhelming piece of moral clockpunching. The exhibit, curator Peter Liebhold told me, "will make people realize that decisions made in government, workplaces and businesses affect other people's lives in ways not apparent at first glance." Given such a ringing sales pitch, tourists could be forgiven for sneaking off around the corner to have a second look at the Swamp Rat Drag Racer.

Between a Rock and A Hard Place is rich in the *thingness* of American history, which is what the Smithsonian does best. Visitors to the NMAH have long paraded back and forth before steam engines, turbogenerators, centrifugal pumps, combines, bridges, the two-story pendulum, and the big locomotives, a great array meant to assure us that our City upon a Hill throbs not merely with republican virtue but with dynaflow generators and internal combustion. The sweatshop hall houses objects of lesser stature and bulk. Among the delights are antique sewing machines, shears and cutters from the turn-of-the-century garment trade, union banners, falsified time cards, massive black-and-white photos of nineteenth century garment factories, clothes made in modern sweatshops, a steel straight-backed chair of the sort that workers fold themselves into for ten- or twelve-hour shifts. The exhibit's centerpiece features reconstructed work stations from the El Monte sweatshop, along with a video in which several workers speak about their ordeal behind its barbed-wire and chain-link fence.

For the most part the exhibit rehearses a fairly standard account of labor history. Sweatshops, we learn, began in the homes of poor and immigrant seamstresses, who worked from dawn to dusk stitching together pre-cut fabric for shop owners. As the industry consolidated, large workloads were contracted out to fly-by-night operators, often im-

migrants themselves, who set up shops in tenement apartments and crumbling walkups all over America's industrial ghettoes. Unions like the Ladies' Garment Workers arose around the turn of the century to challenge the clothing companies on wages, hours and workplace conditions. There were big strikes, and the 1913 fire at the Triangle Shirtwaist Factory in New York—which killed 146 young, mostly Eastern European immigrant women, many of whom were forced to leap from the windows because management kept the doors locked— prompted an outpouring of public disgust and outrage, and eventually led to a number of laws enforcing building codes and workplace inspections. In the Thirties, union organizing and laws enacted under the New Deal combined to virtually stamp out sweated garment production in the United States.

It's a nice story so far. Grandma didn't suffer in vain. Problem is, the march of progress has halted somehow. In the last three decades sweatshops have returned to this country with a vengeance. Here, too, the exhibit does an effective and empathetic job of evoking the busy hands and bent backs of the African-American, Latino and Asian women who replaced Eastern Europeans as the galley slaves of the neoliberal world order.

In fact, this sort of empathy seems to be what museums offer with the most zeal these days. Walking through the Smithsonian in that habitual, sleepy museum daze, one begins to realize that while the exhibit can show us where the bodies are buried, it falters on the crucial matter of apportioning blame. One looks for names to be named but instead finds only vague evocations of a "complex" realm of abstract forces and the vagaries of human nature. In an introductory statement Liebhold remarks that "sweatshops are often discussed as good versus evil, but the issue is much more complex." Nearly the first words out of NMAH Director Spencer Crew's mouth at the opening press conference championed the show's "balanced presentation" of a complicated issue. Balance means, in the evasive language of the exhibit's signage, that manufacturers and retailers don't actively encourage sweated labor, as Lewis Hornthal might have said; they "take advantage" of it.

Curator Harry Rubenstein told me that he and his colleagues had tried to emphasize the way sweatshops have stayed the same over the last 170 years. However, in avoiding detailing and analyzing the economic changes over that period, the exhibit trades a structural argument for an experiential mélange. Often, one is left thinking that it's merely "bad people" who make sweatshops happen. Or, consider such mush as this: "Today's restructuring of the apparel industry is influenced by offshore manufacturing, changes in retailing and inventory practices, and the need to fill orders

quickly." One is left with the impression that sweatshops are a result of, in historian Mike Wallace's words, mere "immanent tendencies" working themselves out, rather than the concerted efforts of the corporate class to increase profits. As with most political discourse these days, analysis of the sustained attack by corporate lobbies on government regulation and union organizing— the two most powerful safeguards against sweatshop abuses—is hardly mentioned, much less evaluated. Little or no attention is given to the garment industry's crackdown on unions, nor to the Taft-Hartley Act, nor to the deregulation craze spurred by corporate lobbies in the last two decades, nor to the defunding of the National Labor Relations Board.

In a telling moment, the El Monte video shows a California law-enforcement official struggling to come to grips with what he views essentially as a civil rights situation, a problem of "human beings enslaving other human beings." Clearly that is the case, but understanding the El Monte sweatshop as *just that* gives us no clue why sweated labor continues to churn out Disney jammies and Nike Air Jordans. People can enslave other people in California today not because some high-minded notion of human rights is missing, but because for more than thirty years the dominant interests in this country have systematically attacked the rights of labor to organize and bargain for decent wages and working conditions.

Occasionally, however, *Between a Rock and a Hard Place* affords glimpses of a workplace horror that the most evasive humanism can't paper over. Barely visible in the lower corner of a display on globalization (which helpfully identifies NAFTA and other free-trade agreements as "influences" on "manufacturers' decisions to source production overseas") is a small reproduction of a 1991 advertisement in *Bobbin*, a garment industry trade magazine. Pictured is one Rosa Martinez, a Salvadoran garment worker who, the ad announces, "you can hire...for 33 cents an hour."

It's a fair bet that if the textile titans have lost any sleep over *Between a Rock and a Hard Place*, it was the thought of Rosa Martinez starting a union, not the Smithsonian's curators, that disturbed their slumber. When word got out of plans for the exhibit two years ago, trade groups such as the American Apparel Manufacturers Association and the National Retail Federation complained, predictably, that sweatshops were not a "suitable" topic for the Smithsonian. More specifically, in the words of the NRF's Pamela Rucker, they felt helpless to "counter the powerful impact of those horrific pictures from El Monte." Naturally, industry lobbyists on Capitol Hill started to bully the Smithsonian into abandoning the show. In the fall of 1997, Ilse Metchek of the California Fashion Association threatened a replay of the Enola Gay imbroglio, in which veterans groups and their allies in Congress browbeat the National Air and Space Museum into bowdlerizing its show on Hiroshima.

Such bravado was as unnecessary as it was fatuous. Within a few months the NRF had changed its mind and even decided to chip into the exhibit. (And why not? It works with Congress.) By the show's opening last April, a "small group" of companies and a trade association, including Levi Strauss, Kmart, Kathie Lee Gifford of Wal-Mart, Malden Mills, and the National Retail Federation, had dropped $76,500 on the show. (By comparison, UNITE kicked in $25,000 and the Labor Department ponied up $5,000, while the Smithsonian itself spent $117,000.) What their money bought them was a few minutes of hopped-up corporate can-doism shamelessly appended to the exhibit as the apparel industry's "perspective" on the sweatshop issue. A promotional video produced by an industry "think tank" called TC^2, running on constant loop, repeats the mantra justifying sweatshop production: Look how much fun life can be for you if you just let the free flow of capital take its course. You being, of course, not a worker but a supplicant to the bounty of commodity fetishism.

A slick piece of work by museum standards, accounting for 15 percent of the show's budget, the video essentially negated the rest of the exhibit. In sharp contrast to the plodding pace and equivocal voice of the other displays, the video beams breathlessly about an exciting, fast-paced garment industry uniting fashion and technology and empowering the hard-working, dedicated people who "make the difference." Those people are, of course, the satisfied and oddly gleeful workers who are pictured operating massive, silent machines in clean, white workspaces, playing volleyball by a manmade office-park lake and getting pumped in a fluorescent company gym. It's all clean white tile, lights and the glamour of the runway and the boutique. Yes, we all eagerly await the day, probably by (when else?) "the year 2000," when we can "walk into our local mall," step into a private booth, have our measurements scanned, select from a menu the look that just happens to complement our very own idiosyncracies, and then saunter home, content that a new self will appear on our doorstep in a few days' time. We can primp, profile, and accessorize, of course, safe in the knowledge that sweated labor (flashing images of a sweatshop in some grainy, low-contrast slum world somewhere not where we are) is a "moral outrage" and a "blight" that responsible manufacturers are hard at work eradicating.

This utterly irrelevant and self-serving buncombe is matched by the obsequious doublespeak in the "statements of concern" that close the show. While UNITE President Jay Mazur and Julie Su, a co-founder of Sweatshop Watch and an adviser to the exhibit, weigh in with attacks on the industry that are quite direct compared to the exhibit itself, Kathie Lee Gifford shamelessly promotes herself and her programs for kids in the ghetto, and Levi Strauss and Kmart tout their voluntary workplace monitoring policies. Maria Echaveste, a representative of President Clinton's sweatshop task force, gravely confirms the administration's commitment to reducing the scourge of sweatshops.

This, then, is balance and complexity at its most sincere: look at the different "opinions," all the perspectives from which to view those embarrassing sweatshops. All things are equal, the forces are all arrayed—just like on the evening news—now go ahead, make up your own mind. As we weigh our options—sweatshops are: a) bad, b) really not that much of a problem, c) unfortunate, d) soon to be a thing of the past, e) a natural feature of the global economy, f) some muddled combination of any of the above—we'd do well to remember that according to the Department of Labor at least half of the nation's twenty-two thousand garment factories in 1996 were in violation of wage and safety laws seriously enough to merit the label "sweatshops." And recently—some nine months after *Between a Rock and a Hard Place* opened—anti-sweatshop forces filed a billion-dollar class-action lawsuit against eighteen major clothing retailers and manufacturers, including Tommy Hilfiger, the Gap, J. Crew, and Wal-Mart. According to the suit, these companies have conspired to keep imported Chinese and South Asian workers in involuntary servitude in sweatshops on the Pacific island of Saipan. For the record, Saipan is a U.S. commonwealth, so anything made there can bear the label "Made in the U.S.A."

It doesn't take much to convince people that sweatshops are morally wrong, but it's quite another thing to reveal the political economy by which seemingly neutral forces shuttle capital and migrant labor across cities, borders, and oceans. As a title, *Between a Rock and a Hard Place* is no doubt intended to describe the dilemma people of good will—in unions, in industry, in government—are supposed to face with regard to sweated labor. But it really captures nothing so well as the Smithsonian's refusal to judge. It's relatively easy to give names to the "rock" and the "hard place" putting the squeeze on the museum—the duties of cultural authority on one hand, the limits of politics on the other—making it unlikely or impossible for this exhibit to truly dissect the sweatshop economy. The forces involved are undoubtedly "complex" in many ways. They involve unknown players, international capital flows, and multiple layers of secrecy that can only have deepened and spread to further reaches of the globe in the years since Lewis Hornthal stonewalled that Gilded Age legislature. But they are hardly unnamable. Just as they did in the last century, the Hornthals of our day count on the fact that public institutions such as the Smithsonian are held in thrall by the bloodless calling of "objectivity" and "balance."

In the most egregious evasion of judgment, the exhibit implies that the final responsibility to bring these latter-day satanic mills to a standstill for good rests with consumers. But as more and more business drifts out to the Caribbean Basin, Southeast Asia, the maquiladoras along the Mexican border, or to any other low-wage, open-shop corporate latifundium with no pesky labor laws or government inspectors (like, apparently, the suburbs of Los Angeles), workers here and abroad do not have the luxury of "balance." They are being brought into new world citizenship not by the abstract order of good-natured objectivity, but with the hard knowledge that they have to choose which side they're on.

PISTOLS FOR TWO
JAY ROSEN VS. THOMAS FRANK

Jay Rosen Writes:

"At a time when the normal condition of the citizen is a state of anxiety, euphoria spreads over the culture like the broad smile of an idiot." The critic Robert Warshow wrote that in 1948. Fifty years later, something similar appears to be on Thomas Frank's mind. Not euphoria, exactly, but a milder mania for "civil society" is leaving its dumb grin on the American scene. I took as much from "Triangulation Nation" (BAFFLER #11), his sharp tale of a fraud case, in which I play some part.

Should you find yourself named in one, an indictment from Frank's pen will have immediate effect, turning your head in its socket a few times before letting go. He is that good a writer. Now he's written against public journalism, which he calls a dim-witted response to escalating troubles in the press. Though the verdict in the end is severe, his essay does a service to public journalism, setting it amid events and eruptions that reach well beyond the news trade. That is where the action is, so here is my reply.

If democracy is a scam, politics a joke, culture a commodity, public discourse a disease, then recent attempts to bring a more "civic" ethic to mainstream journalism must quack like a duck. Quite a sham to start talking about "the American experiment" again, or urge journalists to rejoin it, when the heads of the laboratory are bankrolled to the skies but bankrupt to the core. Here, the remaining task is to connect one odious thing with another, and satirize what passes for seriousness in a jaded age. Frank is good at that.

I wonder, though, what good comes of it, or whether the question even matters to him. (Does it?) In assuming the stance of an "alienated outsider," he seems to reject reform work as either impossible, because conditions are so corrupt, or "infantile," as he calls some of my own phrasings. I was intrigued by that word, since it motions toward what it means to be a grown-up these days. In Frank's view, there is no point in positing a realm between state and market—a civil society—unless you intend to sugarcoat everything and soothe bad conscience all around. What peddlers of middlebrow earnestness mean by "civil this, civil that" is: Don't get too upset, *children*, especially over the ravages of capitalism. Civil society, a "middle-class utopia of order and quiet respectfulness," is a foundation-funded retreat from the real world of markets and money, politics, and power.

Aren't we presented here with the old but not quite exhausted question of working within existing arrangements, so as to get something done vs. standing outside them, so as to offer a more thoroughgoing dissent? And is it true that the only mature choice is the outsider's position? Holden Caulfield thought so, but then he was an adolescent. Frank appears to believe that sophistication in social thought (and journalism) follows from outsiderness. But it doesn't, just as no attempt to work from within is necessarily wise, simply because someone calls it "practical."

Public journalism is a working-within-the-system move. To me, that's no cause to credit or reject it; it's just a description

---

JAY ROSEN teaches journalism at New York University.

of what the thing is. The relevant comparison is to other workable reform schemes, not to a totalizing critique that treats the press as one more feature of the corporate order. For Frank, however, the urgent task is to disable reform: *now*. For nothing will change until we stop talking about changes and see how corrupting and insidious the system is. Worse than those who uphold the status quo are people taking steps toward marginal improvement, because their deceptions are harder to detect than assorted "just do it" campaigns. Co-opting dissent (Frank's *Conquest of Cool*) is the media ironizing itself in order to immunize itself. Since nothing really changes except the ads, the illusion of empowerment is there to be read. A reform effort that aims for modest change is the greater sin, because it says we don't have to wait for critique to take hold before moving forward on some things, in some places. Nike may show towering gall, but piecemeal reform is more galling in its refusal to disable everyone, first.

This isn't to say that no revolutions are needed in the news and information industries. Some are. But it isn't clear how to proceed when the media are in private hands, state funding is out of the question, technology is changing rapidly, and the audience is fragmenting—or being fragged—into lifestyle enclaves. Amid these conditions (revolutionary in their way), journalists find further trouble: Commercial pressures are growing, public trust is evaporating. There's a connection there, but once you've said that, the trick is to find what else to say. I found a single sentence in Frank's essay where he offers journalists a way forward: "Promote local ownership of newspapers somehow, or reduce the power of advertisers, or break up the culture trust, or, at the very least, secure decent wages and working conditions for journalists and pressmen." Fair enough. Shall I expect a future issue of THE BAFFLER on these themes, showing us where and how to begin, or pointing to places where reforms are underway?

Public journalism has come that far, at least. It's not just a series of high-minded phrases without illustration. The illustrations are given, as in my account of the "People Project" in Wichita, which Frank mentions only to make fun of the name. Still, I plead guilty to a certain vagueness in my rhetoric about public journalism. Maddeningly so, in Frank's judgment, necessarily so in mine. "Break up the culture trust" is vague too, but I wouldn't count that against the idea. It's just an idea, until you make common cause with people who can push the notion along. Some may be inside the culture industries, especially if they joined up in hope of doing quality work. Rescuing a culture we can trust from the claws of The Trust can proceed without these people (if you want to risk it), or it can try to move with them. Public journalism has taken the second course, moving with some journalists as they try to puzzle through a loss of authority and the dwindling demand for serious news.

That does not require what Frank condemns: an abandonment of critical judgment to polls and focus groups and marketing gimmicks. But it does mean that judgment in daily journalism (and its power to unsettle things) can be improved if there is sympathy for people's struggle to live public, as well as private lives; a concern for the strength and vitality of civic associations; and a belief that democracy can still work, despite everything arrayed against the prospect. Why all this talk about "listening" to citizens before starting the engines of journalism? Because that's the best way to know where they're coming from, which, clichéd as it sounds, can be helpful if you want a broad public for your best work, and want to address that public on a common plane of understanding—you know, inform people. It is true, as Frank says, that the corporations owning the major news media are unlikely candidates to lead a democratic revival. Equally unlikely, in my view, is the survival of a free and public-spirited press if civil society gets weaker and journalists can do nothing about it.

So what are reporters and editors—not the Gannett Company—supposed to do when a broad public begins to slip from their grasp, when taking the time to read, learn, speak, listen, and get involved appeals to fewer and fewer on the receiving end? We can welcome the delegitimating effects. But as Frank correctly notes, "a nasty legitimacy crisis, a sense of lost authority" has overtaken journalism itself. Is that a good or bad development? I cannot tell from his essay. Nor can I tell if Frank accepts or rejects one premise of public journalism: that there is something worth saving in the American press. A commitment to public service, a native interest in politics and public affairs, a truth-telling spirit among journalists, a quest to enlighten and inform: Are these things real, or just industry pap? Cutting closer to home, are people like Chris Lehmann (a contributing writer for THE BAFFLER, an employee of the publicly traded Times Mirror Company, and a viewpoints editor at *Newsday*) capitalist tools, or can we engage with him and his colleagues on questions of public purpose?

Journalists operate under a host of constraints, including market constraints. They are anxious about public mistrust, worried about the marketeers, and divided about where to go from here. Indeed, they're divided—often bitterly so— about public journalism, which has been condemned from on high as "advocacy" journalism, an abandonment of "objectivity," and a dangerous intrusion of politics into the value-free space of the news. Why? Because it has the gall to treat the press as a political actor, rather than a sideline observer or factory for facts. More room for "civil society" is one thing the actor can act for: now. Not an ideal solution, (or a stop-the-presses critique) but better than "we bring you the world."

Public journalism has also been called what Frank calls it: a sell-out to the Gannetts of our time. Its many doubters doubt it for different reasons. Supporters believe there's a point to be made about the survival of serious journalism and the strengthening of everyday democracy. If that's too vague or too childish for THE BAFFLER and its crowd, then paint an idiot's smile on the thing and you're done. But you may want to consider something before you go: What if democracy is not just a scam, politics not always a joke, culture not only a commodity, public discourse not simply a disease? Under these assumptions (threatening in their way), bitter satire, stylized grievance, and slack-jawed disbelief can still be fun. Just not as baffling.

Thomas Frank replies:

Jay Rosen calls on me to clarify my own critical vision if I'm going to dump on his. So let me start with a simple, practical point: The minimal standard of good criticism, journalism, or history is *getting it right*, reporting in good faith and producing interpretations that correspond in some recognizable way to the known facts. As Rosen knows, we at THE BAFFLER have never been interested in "objectivity." We form our own opinions, we indulge our antipathies, and we aim to pique as well as to entertain. But we try in all circumstances to meet that minimal standard, to get it right. To that end we're less interested in inventing new strategies for market research than we are in describing the world in a manner that is persuasive and that makes sense. We have never been very circumspect about any of these ideas. On the contrary, over the years we have made a number of fairly literal suggestions to journalists on how they might do their jobs better. (See in particular the essays about labor in BAFFLER #9, about the city in BAFFLER #7, and about generational myths in BAFFLER #4.)

But let's hold Rosen's letter up to the same standard. How reasonable is it to describe me as an enemy of democracy generally because I challenged certain very specific reform proposals championed by Jay Rosen? Or to argue that the choice before the nation is either public journalism or revolution? I think most readers are going to spot these fairly quickly as glaring examples of *false opposition*. Likewise, did my story in BAFFLER #11 really argue that public journalism is somehow "worse" than Gannett? Did it really shout, "disable reform: *now*"? Did it really imply that newspaper writers and editors, even ones who contribute to THE BAFFLER, are clueless dupes of their bosses? I think that sensible readers, remembering that in my essay I actually singled out some public journalism projects for praise, that I have gone on the record many times in favor of all sorts of "reforms," and that my writing, too, has appeared in the tainted pages of Times Mirror publications, will dismiss these characterizations of my thinking as *hallucinatory*.

Maybe what Rosen really needs me to do is clarify my argument. I don't object to public journalism because it attempts to "work within the system," but because it fundamentally fails to understand what is wrong with contemporary newspaper writing. Public journalism looks out at the crisis facing newspapers—the public mistrust, the repeated errors, the epidemic failure even to live up to that minimum standard I outlined above—and concludes that the thing to do is to encourage journalists to get in touch with their readers, to discover "where they're coming from." As a reform proposal (or as a rock lyric) this verges on the banal. As a diagnosis of what ails journalism, however, "know your audience" misses the target spectacularly. Editors and publishers still suppress stories for patently ideological reasons, as the *Chicago Sun-Times* demonstrated last year when it killed a profile of Angela Davis. Journalists who venture beyond the pale of "within the system" opinion are still subject to unrelenting condemnation—witness the fates of Gary Webb, who reported on the CIA's connections to drug traffickers, and Robert Parry, who reported on the Iran-Contra affair. And as labor reporting slogs down into the uncomprehending consensus mode (at those papers where it hasn't disappeared altogether), the working conditions for the rest of newspaperdom's inhabitants deteriorate—witness Gannett's recent refusal to take back its locked-out union workers at the *Detroit News* despite a series of court orders commanding them to do so. None of these can really be explained as a failure to understand where readers are coming from, but all make perfect sense when viewed from the perspective I suggest: a critique that takes into account the power of ideology, of moneyed interests, and of social class.

More crucial for our present purposes, though, is the eerie similarity that I pointed out between the standard tools of public journalism—polls, focus groups, town-hall meetings—and the standard tools of marketing. Although Rosen doesn't dispute my argument here, I think it gives context to his comparison of responsible engagement (his strategy) and alienated sniping (mine, apparently). In many cases public journalism doesn't just "work within the system," I pointed out; it actively encourages operations that look and function exactly like traditional audience research. Focus-grouping the news is not a triumph of committed reformers; it's something that even the most bottom-line companies are finding it profitable to do all on their own. To understand such projects as victories of foundation efforts to engage the public strikes me as a rather astonishing reversal of traditional philanthropic priorities. No longer do foundations exist to support worthwhile things that the market has left behind; now they are to be understood as *gratis* think tanks for corporate America.

Rosen's most serious accusation is that I spend comparatively little time proposing real-world solutions to the problems I describe. He implies that criticism is idle unless "you make common cause with people who can push the notion along." Consider, though, that the industry under discussion—the industry to whose salvation I am expected to contribute—is one whose product is criticism, opinion, and expository prose. Newspapers work by informing and persuading; they are, among other things, standing evidence of the materiality of words, the efficacy of written English. It seems odd, to put the kindest spin on it, for a superjournalist like Rosen to assert that shaping opinions through well-reasoned argument, as I attempt to do, is somehow a less legitimate pursuit than shaping opinion through foundation-backed blueprints for the production of feel-good anti-argument. I can't help but wonder what I. F. Stone would think of that.

Bring Us Your Chained and Huddled Masses

Christian Parenti

MASSIVE waves pound the quarter-mile concrete jetty that shelters the bay off Crescent City, California. On either side of the inlet rise small and mangy hills, ravaged by cycles of clear-cut logging. Beneath these slopes is Highway 101 and the gaudy motel-littered strip of a typical California highway town. Miles from nowhere, Crescent City is a working-class burg with middle-class pretensions and aspirations. Normality radiates from its low bungalows, laid out on a bleak and arbitrary grid. Both geography and politics cast a pall over this desolate piece of coast, nestled just below the Oregon border. It's a town only a mayor could love.

Crescent City hasn't had an easy time clinging to normality. With its major industries, timber and fishing, depressed and dying by the mid-Eighties and its economy reeling under the hammer blows of recession, Reaganomics, and globalization, Crescent City was desperate for a new way to finance its version of the American Dream. It found salvation in the arms of the California Department of Corrections (CDC). Today prison is the number one industry in Crescent City and surrounding Del Norte County. Thanks to the sprawling $277 million Pelican Bay State Prison—a "supermax" lockdown renowned as a model of sensory deprivation—a new breed of swine grow fat here on human misery and government cash.

As the same forces that ravaged Crescent City wrought havoc on the rest of the state as well, California's predominantly white and suburban electorate began calling for blood in the "war on crime," the "war on drugs," and also in that thinly veiled war on people of color. This is the context in which Crescent City found its new economic function: Guarding the POWs at Pelican Bay, the place where the faint trail of California justice dead-ends in a sadistic carnival of violence and petty greed.

Outside attention first focused on the new Pelican Bay prison in 1993, when guards forced a raving, shit-smeared inmate—driven nuts by months of isolation in a small white cell—into a tub of scalding water. The prisoner, already dazed, paranoid, and psychotic, was kept in 148-degree water until his skin began to dissolve. He suffered third-degree burns and loss of pigmentation over much of his body. According to documents cited by a federal judge, one of the attending guards commented thusly on the black man's ravaged flesh: "We're going to have a white boy before this is all through."

Madness among inmates at Pelican Bay is epidemic. Over half the prisoners there are deemed "incorrigible," and are locked away in the prison's Security Housing Unit (SHU), a prison within a prison, where inmates are confined to windowless cells twenty-three hours a day. With no work, no education, no communal activity and no recreation (save for one hour a day in an eight-by-twelve concrete box open to the sky) many prisoners break down psychologically. According to human rights investigators, psychiatric care for those thus affected often consists of nothing more than watching cartoons from inside a phone booth-sized cage. Even this sort of "care" is strictly rationed. As a result, convict insanity quickly spins out of control.

"The psychotic inmates are—unequivocally—the most disturbed people I've ever seen," says Terry Kuppers, a veteran psychiatrist and one of the few independent medical experts to have toured the prison's SHU. "They scream and throw feces all over their cells. In a mental hospital you'd never see anything like that. Patients would be sedated or stabilized with drugs. Their psychosis would be interrupted."

But most folks in Del Norte County aren't consumed with sympathy for Pelican Bay's wards. After all, the prison injects more than $90 million a year into the local economy, feeding almost all other economic activity in the region. Town fathers and local boosters view the imported chattel from L.A., Fresno, and Oakland as economic raw material that keeps the town and surrounding county solvent. "Without the prison, we wouldn't exist," says County Assessor Jerry Cochran.

Many suspect that is exactly why the CDC chose Crescent City: Economically weak regions often make gracious hosts for prisons. Hard times, it seems, also have a wonderful way of dulling empathy among the local citizenry. So willing has the town been to accommodate the prison that it sometimes seems like Crescent City has sold its sovereignty to the CDC. Today it is very much a company town, and discipline is its mono-crop.

The county's symbiotic relationship with the prison is most apparent, and appalling, in the local courts. According to research by California Prison Focus (CPF), a human rights group based in San Francisco, even minor disciplinary infractions at Pelican Bay, such as spitting on guards or refusing to return a meal tray, are routinely embellished and prosecuted as felony assault in the local courts. There the mostly black, Latino, and neo-Nazi prisoners face white jurors, who are often friends or family of prison employees.

"From our investigations it seems that the prison, in conjunction with local judges and prosecutors, is using every excuse it can to keep more people locked up for longer," says CPF's Leslie DiBenedetto-Skopek. "It's job security for the whole region."

In other words, the town benefits directly every time a ten-year sentence can be ratcheted up into a twenty- or thirty-year bid. Making matters worse, the CDC pays fully 35 percent of the Del Norte County District Attorney's budget. Given these facts, it is hardly surprising that the citizen-jurors of Del Norte seem to hand out second and third strikes (i.e., life sentences) like lollipops at a bank. Thanks to the demonic economics of incarceration, those who enter Pelican Bay on small-time charges are often trapped permanently inside.

This is the Faustian bargain upon which Crescent City's version of the American dream—its recent affluence and suburban twee—is being built. For their willingness to destroy human lives, the citizens of this county get to enjoy endless government cheese. It is in the town's interest to keep the prison horrific as well: The more inmates who go mad, the more "three strikes" dollars can be channeled north from Sacramento.

Consider the case of Geza Hayes. At age 17, Geza, a white youth from rural Trinity County, got the bright idea of pulling a knife on someone during a brawl. For this Geza received a four-year sentence in the phenomenally brutal Corcoran State Prison. Like most California lockups, Corcoran is Bosnia in a box; a race war managed by local war-lords and their outside allies, i.e., prison gangs and allied guards. Organizations like the Black Guerrilla Family, Nuestra Familia, and the Aryan Brotherhood manage the inside economy, and like feudal barons they wage war and extract money from the masses of inmates in the form of "taxes."

Being white, Geza fell under the jurisdiction of the Aryan Brotherhood. Given the realities of Californian prisons, Geza had three choices. He could "pay taxes" to the mighty AB, he could join them, or he could become another semi-affiliated foot soldier on "the yard." Whether or not Geza joined the AB is unclear, but as far as authorities are concerned he's an AB soldier. For that he was sent to Corcoran's SHU. And that's where Geza's future went through the meat grinder. To leave the SHU, Geza would have had to rat-out other AB soldiers, in a process known as "debriefing." But if he did this and returned to the general population, he would most likely catch a shank in the ribs or worse. So his only real choice was to wait to finish his sentence. But that's easier said than done.

As it turns out, the corrections officers (COs) in the Corcoran SHU had an affinity for Roman games. To break the monotony of watching prisoners slowly go mad, the screws would stage fights between the rival races on the concrete yards of the SHU. Eventually this practice, exposed by the *Los Angeles Times* and the *San Francisco Chronicle*, led to CDC director James Gomez's "reassignment." But the exposés came too late for many.

Geza, who turned nineteen in the abattoir that is the Corcoran SHU, says he was in nine such gladiator fights there. Even having survived these trials, however, he was eventually ensnared in the extreme violence endemic to the SHU. Due to severe overcrowding, Geza found himself double-celled with an alleged AB "snitch." Quite predictably, Geza did what the masters of the AB expected of him: He attacked his new "cellie" with a home-made garrote.

The videotape of the assault, shot by guards preparing to intervene, looks in through the steel mesh door of what appears to be an underground cell. Inside one can make out two pale muscular frames: one twitching limply, the other rippling and shaking with rage, bundled like a human explosive behind the neck of the first. It's clear that Geza has snapped. Then the door slides open, the kevlar-clad screws charge in, and the video stops.

As a result of this incident Geza, only halfway through his four-year sentence, found himself facing new criminal charges in superior court. He plea-bargained, received an additional four years, and was transferred to the very end of the line— Pelican Bay.

Now classified as "extremely violent," Geza was placed in solitary confinement in the Pelican Bay SHU. But due to overcrowding, administrative error, or some malicious subterfuge, another alleged snitch soon landed in Geza's cell. Not surprisingly, Geza again attacked his cellie. He now faces another attempted murder charge.

"I am afraid I'll never get out," Geza says. The young convict from Trinity is now facing his "third strike." If found guilty he will remain in prison for the rest of his life. "I spend a lot of time studying Spanish," Geza explains. "I figure I'll be here for awhile."

One other thing: Every year Geza stays inside costs California taxpayers a bit over $25,000, most of which will end up circulated in Del Norte County.

Targeting Attorneys

THE CDC's influence doesn't stop at the prison walls. Crescent City criminal defense attorneys say that they too are targeted by prison officials, who use behind-the-scenes leverage to prevent effective legal defenses of inmates. "Hell, all I know is that in 1995 I won four out of five of my Pelican Bay cases and they were almost all third strikes—hard cases," booms criminal defense attorney Mario de Solenni, a self-proclaimed "conservative redneck pain-in-the-ass." "Then, in 1996 the judge gave me only one case." According to de Solenni—who owns and drives a large collection of military vehicles—successfully defending prisoners is a no-no in these parts, a taboo that sends authorities far and wide in a search for guaranteed loser lawyers.

"It's bad for the county's economy when the defense wins," agrees another attorney. Numerous Crescent City defense lawyers tell similar stories of beating the prosecution too many times and then finding themselves with no defense appointments. If they want to continue practicing criminal law they often end up leaving town.

Jon Levy, who holds a correspondence law degree, used to make his living defending Pelican Bay inmates charged with committing crimes inside prison. "I don't do defense anymore," says the nervous, balding Levy as he walks his small dog along the rubble-strewn beach. After winning a few cases Levy was cut off; the judges stopped assigning him work. "I can't make a living here. Even if I switched to civil cases, all my potential clients work for the prison." Levy is, quite literally, a victim of a company town blacklist. And he's not alone.

Tom Easton, a genteel civil rights attorney with the slightly euphoric air of someone who's just survived a major auto wreck, lives with his Russian wife in a modest house overlooking the sea on the north side of town. *The National Review* and *American Spectator* cover his coffee table, but right-wing reading habits haven't endeared him to the CDC compradors. "The prison and the DA are trying to destroy my career," says Easton with a vacant smile. Until recently Easton faced several felony charges, including soliciting perjury from a prisoner, arising from his defense of Pelican Bay inmates. He says the charges were nothing more than retaliation for providing an effective defense in criminal cases and handling civil rights suits on behalf of convicts. Eventually all the charges against Easton were dropped, reversed, or ended in hung juries. "But the DA could still try to have me disbarred," says

Easton. In the meantime, he has been banned from communicating with the seven Pelican Bay prisoners he represents.

Easton's sin was that he strayed from his permitted role as provider of the mandatory feeble defense, and even dared to file a few civil suits on behalf of maimed and tortured prisoners. "I am convinced they're going after Easton because he helped prisoners," says Paul Gallegos, a defense attorney, who, like others representing Pelican Bay convicts, has been harassed by the DA.

Carceral Keynesianism

WHAT'S going on in Crescent City isn't just free-floating meanness. The town's culture of civic sadism appears to be the deliberate result of state policy. Economic troubles began here in the Sixties, when the salmon and timber industries, long the lifeblood of the region, began to sputter. Then in 1964 a massive tsunami rolled in and crushed Crescent City's quaint downtown. Only nine people died, but the place never fully recovered. After the waters receded the local planners carried on as best they could, and bulldozed the old town center's twisted rubble across Highway 101 into the sea—where it still forms a contorted barrier of sidewalk slabs, tiled bathroom walls, and buckled asphalt. In place of the old redwood Victorians, a cheap and shabby imitation of Southern California was erected: minimalls, covered open-air walkways, empty parking spaces, dingy box-like motels.

By the early Eighties Crescent City's economy—part of the Golden State only in name—was hemorrhaging badly. All but a handful of the area's sawmills had been shut down, commercial salmon fishing finally died, and businesses collapsed by the hundreds. The small businessmen and real estate boosters who ran the place made a clumsy series of attempts to "reposition" the regional economy. Like other towns, Crescent City latched on the idea of becoming a tourist destination. And as so often happens, the strategy failed, in part because of the region's isolation and its unfortunate, newly built environment. The tourism strategy ultimately produced a few motels now used only by long haul truckers and a hulking botch of a "convention center."

By 1989 unemployment reached 20 percent and population was declining. Crescent City and Del Norte County had sunk into a seemingly terminal economic torpor. Enter the California Department of Corrections, the knight in khaki armor, searching for a site to build a new mega-dungeon. Like any battered and anemic damsel in distress, the local boosters saw their chance: The region would move from exporting fish and trees to importing brown people and renegade white trash. From now on, the town's fate would be tied to the weighty task of justice, its civic culture remade to reflect that somber mission. Facing little opposition the CDC moved in, commandeered some unincorporated land outside of town and set about building the state's most feared lockup.

For the most part, the Faustian bargain has paid off. Del Norte County is, in its own distorted way, booming. Pelican Bay provides 1,500 jobs, an annual payroll of $50 million and a budget of over $90 million. Indirectly, the concrete beast at the edge of town has created work in everything from construction to domestic-violence counseling to drug-dealing. The contract for hauling away the prison's garbage alone is worth $130,000 a year—big money in the state's poorest county. With the employment boom came almost 6,000 new residents. In the last ten years the average rate of housing starts has doubled, as has the value of local real estate.

The prison's economic wake washed in a huge Ace Hardware, a private hospital, and a 90,000-square-foot Kmart, selling everything from toothpaste to Pocahontas pajamas. Across from Kmart is an equally gargantuan and bleak Safeway. "In 1986 the county collected $73 million in sales tax; last year it was $142 million," says the gung-ho County Assessor Jerry Cochran. On top of that, local gov-

ernment is saving money by replacing public works crews with low-security "level-one" prisoners. Between January 1990 and December 1996, Pelican Bay inmates worked almost 150,000 hours on everything from school grounds to public buildings. According to one report, if the prison labor had been billed at the meager sum of $7 an hour, it would have cost the county at least $766,300.

Similar scenarios have been replicated scores of times in recent years. From Bowling Green, Missouri to Green Haven, New York, economically battered small towns are putting out for new prisons. And they end up paying for economic safety in ways they never imagined. They are beset not only by overloaded sewer systems but overburdened social services agencies, as whacked-out wives, children, and corrections officers stumble in, reeling from work-related stress, abuse, and addiction. But out here, Middle America's thirty-year-old backlash and its lust for punishment means just one thing: jobs. Acc '-ng to the National Criminal Justice Commission, 5 percent of the growth in rural population between 1980 and 1990 is accounted for by prisoners, captured in the inner city and transported out to the to new carceral Arcadia.

The Keynesian stimulus that is awarded to prison towns does not, of course, explain the whole criminal justice crackdown. Ultimately, the Big Round-Up is a way of managing the renewed inequality of American capitalism, which is itself the result of the intensified quest for corporate profits—a crusade that became all the more desperate after the social and economic crisis of the early Seventies.

It's also the byproduct of politicians' endless search for compelling issues that don't address the realities of class power and exploitation. Crime mobilizes voters in a very safe way. And building prisons isn't a bad way to dole out the federal pork that—editorial hosannas about American entrepreneurialism notwithstanding—has always been the driving economic force in American capitalism.

The CDC eats its own

PRISONERS and their defense attorneys aren't the only ones in Crescent City who are apparently targeted by CDC skulduggery. Even screws who take the job seriously find themselves in trouble.

John Cox looks like a poster boy for the CDC. But the six-foot-four, ruddy-faced, former Pelican Bay CO is on the prison's shit-list. Trouble began in 1991 when Cox broke the guards' code of silence and testified against a fellow officer who had beaten an inmate's head with the butt of a gas gun, and then framed the victim. Cox refused to go along with yet another set-up. According to findings in *Madrid v. Gomez*—a high-profile class action suit against the CDC—Pelican Bay administrators called Cox a "snitch" and told him to "watch his back."

But even before Cox broke ranks in court he was hated by other guards. "I gave all my officers 100 extra hours of on-the-job training beyond the standard forty," explains Cox with evident pride. But his behavior as sergeant in charge of the D-yard SHU was seen as treachery by many hard-line COs. "They called D-Yard SHU 'fluffy SHU,' because we didn't hog-tie inmates to toilets or kick in their teeth after cell extractions," says Cox. Trying to explain the CO subculture, Cox relates: "There was one officer in there who used to take photos of every shooting and decorate his office with them. For some of them it was Vietnam or something."

In Pelican Bay's slow-motion riot of sadism and corruption, Cox—trying to play by the rules—found it almost impossible to do his job. "I broke up one fight without assistance, called for backup but none came, and got a torn rotator cuff," says Cox. "The next day the lieutenant made me climb every guardtower ladder. It was pure harassment." The final straw was a series of death threats and close calls on the job. In one incident Cox found himself alone, surrounded by eight inmates, and unable to get backup. "That was it. If I stayed and tried to do my job I probably would have been killed," says Cox, who is currently suing the CDC.

Things have hardly improved since Cox quit: "Bullets through the windows, death threats sent to my kids, hang-up calls, sugar in the gas tank, slashed tires, you name it." According to Cox, the DA and the sheriff have refused to investigate these allegations. "They told me to talk to the prison," he says. Officials at Pelican Bay refuse to comment on Cox's case. But Tom Hopper,

former Del Norte County sheriff and the current community resource manager at Pelican Bay, did offer these barely coded remarks: "The prison saved this community and people are grateful. There are a few disgruntled employees and other fringe elements that complain, but you can't please everybody."

Even prison maintenance workers who testified against administrators in a recent corruption case say they've been harassed. "The former head of operations out there made death threats against my clients, and the state is still investigating," says lawyer Levy, who defended one of the maintenance workers. His client has since been forced to leave town after being fired from the local hardware store, allegedly at the behest of a prison official. "The prison is the only place that buys in bulk," explains Levy. "So suggestions by its officials are as good as direct orders as far as small businesses are concerned."

The evil juggernaut of prison power gets even weirder. The CDC has covert investigative units that conduct surveillance in communities near prisons and keep dossiers on local troublemakers. "Internal Affairs does investigations in the community, but I don't think that's inappropriate," says Tom Hopper. Corrections officials in Sacramento also confirm that the department's two undercover police forces do at times carry out surveillance outside prison grounds. During recent revelations of officially sponsored violence at Corcoran State Prison, officers from one of those units were caught trying to intimidate

whistleblowers. They even went so far as to chase down one guard as he raced to the FBI with videotapes of the Corcoran gladiator fights.

The damage from Crescent City's latest tsunami—rule by the CDC—isn't limited to the shattered lives of inmates, whistleblowers, and lawyers. Though prison is often sold as a "clean industry," it does bring with it what economists call "externalities" and "diseconomies." In manufacturing, the externalities are things like pollution. But in the prison business they are madness and violence. Two years ago an inmate was released directly from the Pelican Bay SHU to the local bus station. He was found two days later, half way to his hometown, splattered in blood, having raped a woman and put a hammer through her head.

So while capitalism restructures—driving down wages, breaking unions, decimating cities in the name of austerity and profits—a new niche market arises. The business of disciplining the surplus populations of the post-industrial landscape becomes a way of reincorporating the enraged remnants of middle America. Small cities from Bedford Falls to Peoria must become the Vichy regimes of fortress capitalism, they must "reinsert" themselves on the winners' terms, or they must wither and die. Today, Middletown's "comparative advantages" are the fury that receding prosperity has engendered and a cruelty sufficient to process the social wreckage of capital's great march forward. The diseconomies of economic restructuring are recycled into politically useful raw material: Dislocation brings rage, and rage contains the dislocation, each movement in the process lubricated with a stupefying political silence.